# FAE PTA

Uncle Chip Saves the Fae
Book 2

## JAMIE DAVIS

MedicCast Productions

**Fae PTA**

**By Jamie Davis**

Copyright © 2023 by Jamie Davis. All rights reserved.

Cover design by CoversByChristian.com

This is a work of fiction. Any resemblance to actual persons living or dead, businesses, events, or locales is purely coincidental.

Reproduction in whole or in part of this publication without express written consent is strictly prohibited. The author greatly appreciates you taking the time to read his work. Please consider leaving a review wherever you bought the book, or telling your friends about it, to help him spread the word.

Thank you for supporting his work.

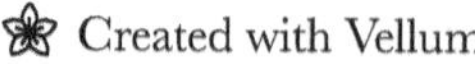 Created with Vellum

# Acknowledgments

This book made possible with the generous assistance of these Kickstarter Backers:

Kristi Preston-Barnes, Dom Graham, Jessica Spring, Martha Carr, Conrad J, Nic Anderson, Glen Errington, Christian "Mecki" Hejl, Gerald P. McDaniel, Ryan Scott James, Delia A Landstrom, Arveyah Wright, Merri, Brianna Welch-Martin, E.M. Middel, Mary Eleanor, Kathy D C, Deborah Snowden, Dr. Cindy Ann Simon, Rabbi Fred Natkin, Beth Jones, Carol Cha, Rec, Sue Byrne, Karen Johnson, Stephen Ballentine, Melinda Kucsera, Scott McConnell Distance CME, Sabrina Graham, Nan & Rick W., Jenn Mitchell, Renee Roberts

# Chip

The quarterstaff swept around in a broad arc, moving faster than I would have thought possible. I made a half attempt at leaping over it as it dipped low, aiming for my shins.

I almost made it.

The staff cracked against my left leg just above my ankle. The force of the blow took my feet out from under me. I crashed to the floor. The landing knocked the wind from me in an oof of air rushing out of my lungs.

I couldn't afford to relax, despite being out of breath and nursing an injured ankle. My opponent wouldn't let up one bit. Knowing the next attack was already on its way, I rolled over to the right twice and pushed up onto my knees.

My own staff lay on the floor close by, but it would take too much time to get it. I pushed off to the side to dodge once again.

The iron shod butt of my opponent's weapon stomped down only an inch from my side. I'd moved just in time. I avoided the end of the staff but wasn't quick enough to avoid the booted foot or the kick to my midsection that flipped me over onto my back. A second later I stared at the metal-wrapped butt of the quarterstaff hovering in front of my face.

I traced my eyes up the shaft to the manicured fingers holding the wooden weapon, then on up to the piercing emerald eyes glaring down at me.

"You win again, Rose."

She lowered the staff and set the end on the floor next to her as she stood up straight from her fighting stance. "You're still falling for the feint, Chip. You've got to learn not to do that. I get you almost every time with that trick. It's been two years since you became the Guardian. When are you going to start paying attention?"

I sat up, rubbing at my bruised ribs. I'd had martial arts training from many good teachers over the years, but none of them were as brutal as Rose Eldersdottir, my sister-in-law, and the weapons master of the Fae family my brother, Bobby, had married into. Ever since his death two years before alongside his wife, Lili, I'd been designated as Guardian to their two children, Sadie and Addison. I still heard the capital G in that word. It was because six-year-old Sadie was the future Fae queen, if she lived to see eighteen.

"I tried to avoid the follow-up attack. It was an attempt to make you think I fell for the feint."

Rose scowled. "How'd that work out for you, Chip? You've got to pay attention. Someday, you might be in a fight without me close by to save you."

"Hey, I held my own. My Guardian powers were enough to ward off the attacks we've had so far."

There'd been a few attempts to get at Sadie and Addison, especially a particularly deadly attempt by a killer-witch nanny I hired by accident. I learned that lesson quickly enough. After that, there were a few things that Rose called probing attacks, but nothing serious enough that I even saw the attackers.

"Maybe they've given up. We haven't had anyone try to get to the kids in almost a year."

"This is too important for anyone to relax. I promise you, Chip. Whoever it is who knows Sadie's secret, they're not standing down. I'm worried they're just marshaling their forces until they see an opening. That's the reason you have to train and train again. You have to be at your best every time. They only have to get through you once to succeed."

I stood and winced a little when I put weight on my bruised ankle. Rose crossed to the rack of weapons and settled the quarterstaff in a slot so it leaned upright against the wall. I retrieved my staff from the floor and put it next to hers.

Rose fetched her shining silver sword from the stand on the table by the door. "Let's try some maneuver and flexibility drills. Get a wooden practice sword from the rack and join me in the middle of the floor."

I moved down the weapons rack to a large selection of weighted wooden blades of different designs. I chose one modeled to imitate a standard medieval longsword. After hefting the blade for a few practice swings, I knew it was heavy enough to give my muscles the intended workout.

"Come on, Chip. We don't have much time left. Aunt Allura only agreed to watch the kids for two hours."

I walked to the center of the room to stand an arm's length away from her. "I don't know what the fuss is. It's not like she's watching them. She's either got her housekeeper doing it or Reston is tending to them while he does whatever a Fae butler does."

"That's not the point. Being true to your word is something Allura takes seriously. If we said two hours, she'll expect us to honor the agreement."

The regular sitter for our training days was out of town visiting her sick mother. Rose had finally relented when I asked for the hundredth time to hire a part-time sitter for afternoons a few times a week and the occasional evening out.

The sitter, a dryad named Sammi Sinclair, had passed Rose's extensive background checks. She also came highly recommended by her older sister, a state park ranger we'd met soon after I became the Guardian. That same park ranger had helped save all our lives during the first major attack on Sadie I'd encountered after taking on my new role.

I raised my sword up at arm's length in front of me, the end pointed up at a forty-five-degree angle. "I'll be glad when Sammi gets back. We need to be back in the routine again with school starting soon for Sadie."

Rose started a slow and purposeful series of moves. She led with her blade, but the motions involved her entire body. I emulated her moves as best as I could, though I was sure I'd never match her lithe, supple motions completely. Watching her toned, athletic body beside me distracted me from what I was doing, and I lost balance. I had to step to the side to recover.

"Focus, Chip. That's your number one problem. You don't pay close enough attention to the details I'm trying to teach you."

I returned to my position and rejoined the training kata with Rose. I don't know why she always distracted me that way. It wasn't like I had those kinds of feelings for her. That ship had sailed when we hooked up the one and only time at Bobby and Lili's wedding reception. Since then, we've had a platonic, though often adversarial, relationship. It was only put aside when it came to taking care of the kids, to which we both had devoted our lives.

Concentrating, I moved through the positions, the weighted wooden blade taxing my muscular arms beyond what an actual blade would do. I knew it was to increase my stretch and muscle memory, but it still hurt like hell for a few days after our sessions.

We wove through the patterns in slow, deliberate motions for fifteen minutes. Even Rose was glistening with sweat by the time we were finished. I was drenched, soaking through my T-shirt and in desperate need of a shower. A check of the clock on the wall told me we didn't have the time to spare, though. Rose was right about Allura. The elder matriarch of the Fae royal family in hiding wouldn't tolerate tardiness as a reason for breaching an agreement.

I returned the sword to the weapons stand and rolled my shoulders to try and loosen them up. I could use a good post-workout stretch, but there was no time. Rose sheathed her long silver blade and grabbed the small purse and keys from the table by the door. The dojo belonged to a friend of hers. He let her use it to train me before and after it opened for regular students. The guy was a type of Unusual, but I wasn't sure what kind. Even after two years of awareness about the hidden

Unusual world of the supernatural all around us, I still had trouble recognizing them from among the human counterparts living and working beside them.

Rose held the door and let out an exasperated sigh. "Chip, come on. We've got to get all the way across town to my aunt's place."

"I'm coming. You're the one who whacked my ankle with the staff."

"Move faster now or block the attack next time. Get in the car."

I climbed into the passenger side of her candy-apple red Firebird. It was a fully restored version from the late eighties. I'd barely buckled the seat belt before she peeled out of the parking space and sped into traffic. Next time, I was definitely driving. Usually I met her here, but she'd met us at Aunt Allura's place and insisted on driving rather than taking two cars.

She wove in and out of traffic like a wild woman until we were outside of town and heading into the farmland outside of Westminster, Maryland. Allura's horse farm nestled in the hills to the northwest of town. Soon we drove down the long lane lined with white board fences on either side. Rose had slowed to a more normal pace. Her aunt would not appreciate having Rose arrive at her normal driving speed.

We got to the door just in time. My phone showed it had just ticked over to the top of the hour. Sadie came to the door with Reston, the Butler. She stood about waist high now that she was six, with long black hair that was braided into two pigtails hanging down across her shoulders.

"Uncle Chip!" She rushed out to hug me. She immediately let go. "Ew, you're all sweaty and wet."

"Sorry, kiddo. Aunt Rose worked me hard today."

"Don't listen to him, Sadie," Rose said. She winked at her niece. "He's just a big baby, like all men."

Sadie giggled and tugged at my hand to come inside. "Addy's back helping the cook with a batch of cookies. You can try the ones we've already baked."

I let the little girl pull me back through the mansion until we reached the large kitchen in the back. Addy, who'd just turned three, knelt on a tall chair beside the cook. He had flour smudged on his face amidst his light brown hair.

"Unca Chip." He called. "I make cookies."

"I see that, Addy. I hope you're being a good help to Ms. McGarry."

"He's being a very good boy. He wanted to help break the eggs, but we discovered opening the butter was a better chore for little boys, didn't we." The jolly, rotund woman had a twinkle in her eye as she patted Addy on the back.

"I'm glad watching him wasn't too much trouble," I said. "They were both good?"

"Of course," she replied. "It's been too long since we've had little ones running around here. I still remember Lili and Rose chasing each other through these halls. The laughter of tiny voices brightens the heart."

I tried not to react to Ms. McGarry's mention of remembering Rose and Lili as kids. She didn't look old enough to be around that long ago. Still, I knew some Fae varieties aged slower than humans did, so I really had no idea how old she was. It made me wonder how old Allura must be to have the all the wrinkles and gray hair she had.

As if she knew I was thinking about her, Aunt Allura entered the kitchen. The permanent disapproving frown sat ever-present on her face. "At last, you've returned, Rose. The noise of these children has made it hard for me to rest upstairs."

"We said two hours and that's exactly how long we were gone, Aunt Allura," Rose replied.

The old woman sniffed with her nose in the air. "Well, I'm glad you've come back to retrieve them. How is the Guardian's training coming along?"

It annoyed me how she ignored my presence sometimes. Even though she supported Lili and Bobby's wishes to include me as the Guardian in their wills, she had never warmed up to me. It had been a point of pride for a long time, and I took it personally. Women generally loved me. Except Rose, of course. And her Aunt Allura, too, apparently. Maybe it was a Fae thing.

"Sadie, say goodbye to your two aunts and thank Aunt Allura for helping watch you."

Sadie ran first to Rose and wrapped her arms around her hips. "Love you, Aunt Rose."

"Love you, too, Sadie. Take care of Addy for me until I see you again. You're almost a big girl now."

"I am a big girl already. I'm going to be in first grade."

"Yes, you are," Rose answered.

Sadie turned and solemnly faced Aunt Allura. She carefully curtsied just the way I'd showed her. "Goodbye, Aunt Allura."

We'd been working on this all week. I'd hoped it would show Allura I was honoring their Fae traditions. All we got in return was another sniff that might have been approval. I wasn't sure.

"Come on, kids. Let's load up and get home. I want to get some work around the house done before dinner time."

"Can we take some of the cookies with us, Uncle Chip?" Sadie asked. "We worked hard on them."

"That's up to Ms. McGarry."

The cook winked at me and produced a zippered plastic bag of cookies all ready to go. I took the bag with a quick thank you and herded the kids towards the front door. Rose came right behind me. Reston waited at the entrance until we all left and then closed the door with a resounding thump.

I shrugged and smiled at Rose. "Okay, kids, load up the van. It's time to go."

I had kept Lili's minivan, mostly because the kids had been comfortable traveling in it after their parents died. Now, it had become my favorite mode of transport around town. It was perfect for hauling the kids and held more groceries than my Tesla did. I helped clip Addy into his car seat and checked to make sure Sadie was all buckled into her booster seat.

Rose walked with me around to the driver's side of the van. It was on the way back to her Firebird. "Sammi is supposed to be back from seeing her mother in a few days. Do you want to schedule another session now or wait until you hear from her when she gets home?"

"We can meet at the regular time in two days. I should be sufficiently recovered by then to take you on again." One thing about being the Guardian, I'd found I healed up faster than ever before. At one point during a training session a few months before, I'd broken my arm. It was back in action within a week and a half. Rose had called it a side effect of the old magic that had sealed my position in the family.

"That works, but we can't ask Aunt Allura to watch them again. We've used up that avenue."

"I could ask Barbara or Ellie across the street to watch them for a few hours. Surely the kids would be safe there. We've known them long enough now to know they're nothing more than suburban soccer moms."

Rose started to say something in reply, then stopped herself. After a few seconds, she said, "I suppose I could slip over there tonight or the next and put up some basic wards around their houses, too. We wouldn't be far away, and I'd know instantly if trouble happened."

My eyebrows shot up in shock. "I'm sorry, who are you and what have you done with the real Rose?"

"Very funny. At some point, we're going to have to let the kids go out in the world a little more. Addy is getting old enough to start some sports and Sadie starts first grade in a few weeks." She shook her head. "I don't like it, but it's the truth. I'm working on having a few charms made up for them to wear so we can find them if they're in trouble away from home. The magic will also offer some basic protection from some harmful spells and magic."

This was the first I'd heard of the new charms. "When were you going to tell me about these charms, Rose? We agreed to tag team on this stuff. You're supposed to keep me in the loop when you come up with a new security measure so I can weigh in. Besides, I don't need a charm to find Sadie. I can sense where she is all the time already."

"Okay, I'm telling you now. Plus, I don't have that ability. That's a Guardian thing. Do you approve or not?"

"I suppose so. How big are they going to be?"

Rose held up her hand and made a tiny circle with her thumb and forefinger about the size of a dime. "Not big at all. They can wear them on a chain or even a simple leather thong around his wrist in Addy's case."

"Okay, I guess that's fine. But tell me next time you have these kinds of ideas."

Rose nodded and headed back to her car with a wave over her shoulder at me. "I'll let you know when I have them made."

I climbed into the minivan and watched as Rose pulled away. Despite our improved working relationship, she still constantly did things that got under my skin. I wondered if that would ever get better as I drove down the driveway on the way home.

# 2

# Rose

I looked up in my rear-view mirror to watch the van following me down the lane at my aunt's place. Chip always acted like he was in charge. He made sure he had the final say about the simplest things I did to protect the kids. It wasn't like I was going to do anything that would endanger them. Lots of Unusual kids wore protection charms when away from their parents. It helped protect them from detection by the oblivious humans in the world around them. Sadie and Addy deserved them as much as most normal Unusual kids.

My white-knuckled grip on the steering wheel showed my annoyance. I found myself wanting to take Chip back to the dojo and beat my feelings out of him again like I did earlier.

I took a deep breath. I didn't know why I let him get under my skin the way I did. Besides, his request to know more about the charms before I had them made was a reasonable one, as much as I hated to admit it.

There was another reason I wanted to see the old smith at the county Farm Museum. In addition to fashioning simple brass charms for folks around the community, he also had a hidden talent most didn't know about. He'd been trained by some of the most skilled blade smiths from the old country before he moved to America almost a century before. He was the perfect person to make a blade fit for a Queen's Guardian. I definitely didn't want Chip learning about this until I got everything lined up. It was supposed to be a surprise.

Chip had been working on honing his Guardian skills, but the one thing he lacked was a weapon worthy of a protector like himself. Even in the modern world we lived in, he deserved a blade made by a master smith and imbued with the proper magics to align with his Guardian powers. That was something only a smith as skilled as this one could do. There were many others up to making basic protection charms. Those were just an excuse to bring up the weapon.

At the end of Allura's lane, I turned right while Chip and the minivan turned left to head back into town. Once out on the main road, I punched the accelerator and zoomed down the back country roads to get to my appointment with the smith. I got to the gravel lot outside the museum property just in time. I flashed my annual pass to the person at the gate and went inside. I made a beeline for the smithy attached to the large barn behind the old stone farmhouse.

The steady ringing of metal on metal emanated from the doorway. The forge fire inside lit up the interior with an orange and yellow glow. The hammering stopped and the smith used the tongs to shove the bar of iron back into the coals. He reached up and pumped the bellows a few times to heat up the coals once more and waited.

The man behind the bellows stood barely five feet tall. His shoulders stretched out so broadly they gave the impression of having a span matching his height. His long brown and gray beard hung down and tucked into the broad leather belt at his waist. That same belt secured the thick leather apron around his considerable middle section. The humans might think him an odd sort of fellow, which he was, for a human. To the Unusual community, the smith represented a classic mountain dwarf in every way.

When he saw me standing watching from the doorway, he inclined his head and said, "Welcome, Princess. What brings you back to my forge? I have not yet crafted the two amulets you asked for. That will take more time than just a few days, I'm afraid."

"I actually came back about something else." I leaned back out the entrance to make sure no one lurked outside the smithy. I stepped back inside, and beads of perspiration popped up on my exposed skin from the heat in the enclosed space.

"Oh, what else is it that you need?"

"I did some checking around. I found out you are a master blade-smith. Is that true?"

The smith's forehead creased in concern, and he frowned. "I have not been a bladesmith for a very, very long time. I no longer make weapons of war and death. I think you should seek out such a thing from somewhere else. Don't you already have a fine blade of your own?"

"I do," I replied. "But it's not for me. It is for a very special human who needs a weapon to go along with his unique skillset."

The smith barked a laugh. "Now I know you are crazy. I would never make a weapon of power for a human to use. They only relish power for power's sake. They have no understanding of the meaning of wielding powerful magic."

"This one is no ordinary human. Every day he gains more knowledge of our world as he takes a journey he didn't choose for himself. He has been granted the powers of a Guardian. He is struggling to understand his magic and I believe that is due to his lacking a weapon suitable to someone given that important duty. He needs to become a champion and needs a blade to match."

"Hmmmm." The smith's nonresponse caught me by surprise. He reached into the coals with his metal tongs and removed a glowing yellow bar of iron. He laid it on the black anvil and picked up a large hammer.

Clang, clang, clang.

He turned the bar on its side. Its glow had cooled to a deep red by now.

Clang, clang, clang.

The process repeated itself numerous times. Heat and hammer, heat and hammer, until it had grown dark outside.

With a final twist of his body, the smith shoved the flattened bar back into the coals. He set the tongs down on the anvil beside the hammer and looked up at me in the glow of the forge's light.

"I'll think on it."

A grin slipped onto my face. I hid it behind a hand until I could regain control of my emotions again.

"I'll not be rushed in this decision. It is not an easy life to return to, the forging of weapons. They take a price from inside you much like the price of the lives they may destroy someday."

I inclined my head. "I will wait for you to decide then. Shall we proceed to talking some about the magical elements needed for the charms you promised me instead?"

The smith grumbled. "Bah, the charms you ask for are nothing but simple baubles. I have most of what I'll need already. There may be other things required, though. What specific protections and powers did you wish to infuse into the alloy?"

I pondered the question. I'd known I wanted a charm for each of the kids, but now I was faced with the choices involved, I found myself unprepared to make a decision about them.

As I thought about each of the children and who they might become someday, a few choices slipped into my mind. "For the first, agility of mind and body. It must deflect coercion and influence magic as well."

The old dwarf nodded and returned to staring at me, awaiting my next response.

"For the other, I need strength of muscle and character. It must also inspire loyalty in those who would follow."

"Those are powerful magics. The metals involved in the alloys to use them are rare and difficult to procure, even in this modern age of one-day delivery. I cannot just pull out my phone and use an app to order them. It will take time."

"How much time?" I asked.

"Two weeks, I think. Yes, that will be enough time for the gathering and the forging."

I thought about the pending school year starting in two weeks. "You have a week and a half. Can you do it in that time?"

The smith offered a slight bow. "It will be as you request, Princess. The charms will be ready for you to pick up in ten days." He picked up the tongs without saying anything else and returned to his work.

Clang, clang, clang. Turn the metal. Clang, clang, clang.

Realizing the smith had finished talking for the night, I nodded once and left him to his work. The cool night air wicked away the perspiration from my skin as soon as I left the intense heat of the forge. Goosebumps rose on my arms and neck and sent a shivering chill down my spine. I didn't mind, though. I had gotten what I had come to get.

I had no doubt the smith would eventually give in and forge a weapon for Chip, one worthy of a Guardian. I would also have the magical charms for the children before Sadie started school. Giving them the charms this early in life offered the added benefit of infusing some of the magic from them directly into the children's being. Later in life, even without them, each would be more agile and stronger than others like them. It could mean the difference between life and death.

It was almost eight o'clock when I reached the Farm Museum's front gate. I was among the last of the day's visitors to exit the living history museum. Perhaps when it was time to pick up the charms, Chip and I could return with the children. They would enjoy the petting zoo and the other children's exhibits.

With school just around the corner, though, there was a lot to do and Chip probably had the next two weeks blocked out with school shopping for Sadie. I made a mental note to check in with him so I didn't assume the kids were free when they weren't. These last two years since he became the children's legal guardian and Sadie's magical Guardian, Chip had done a decent job raising the kids. I made the admission begrudgingly, but it was the truth. He didn't do things exactly the way I always wanted him to do it, but for the most part, the results were the same.

I got in my car and decided to go and grab a bite to eat and enjoy the rest of the evening at home. There were always more things that needed doing than there was time in the day. The trick was to know when to stop and take a break at the end of the day. For me, after dealing with both Chip and my aunt, I decided the workday was over. Time to get some rest.

3

# Chip

I checked the backpack full of kid supplies for the day's outing. Rose had something important to do with the children, although she didn't tell me all the details. It had something to do with a blacksmith who worked locally. This weekend, he was plying his ancient trade down at the Maryland Ren Faire in Crownsville. It was about an hour away, over near Annapolis, the state capital.

"Addy, go and get your shoes. I'll help you put them on. Aunt Rose is almost here." The toddler waddled off into the kitchen where a shelf with cubby holes had spots for the kid's shoes, hats, and gloves. He came back with a pair of sneakers that lit up in flashing red LEDs whenever he took a step. They were his current favorite things in the world.

"Light up shoes?" He asked, holding them up for me.

I took the shoes and then picked him up to set him on the edge of the dining room table so I could reach his feet more easily. I slipped the shoes on the tiny feet and closed the tabs that held them tight.

"All set, little guy. Go look out the window with Sadie for Aunt Rose to get here. I'll be right there after I load up a few things into the van." I ran through a mental checklist almost automatically now whenever I took the kids out of the house. Addy was in pull-up diapers.

From everything I could see, he was nowhere near ready to potty train at almost three. Ellie across the street had commented about boys and their little fire hoses taking longer to learn that particular skill. I couldn't wait to have him out of diapers. It would make leaving the house much easier.

I took the backpack diaper bag out to the car, picking up their cups full of water for the ride on my way through the kitchen to the garage. I put the diaper bag in the back with the stroller and set the cups in the holders in each kid's car seat. I returned to shouts from little voices in the hallway.

"Addy, you have to listen to me. I'm going to be your Queen someday."

"No. You Sadie. Not Queen."

"What seems to be the problem here, Sadie?"

She pointed at the front bay window in the living room. "He pulled on the curtains to climb up onto the front windowsill. I told him he wasn't allowed up there."

I looked at Addy, standing in a defiant pose in the middle of the hallway with his little fists balled up. He looked as determined as he did about everything right now. He had definite opinions about things and how they should be. I'd had to start using the timeout chair more frequently in recent weeks. Addy pushed back on just about everything.

"Addy, you are not allowed up into the bay window. You know that."

"I not see."

"You could climb in the chair by the window like you usually do to look outside," I suggested.

He looked like he was working up to a full-blown temper tantrum. However, Aunt Rose arrived to save the day by distracting the kids from their argument.

"Aunt Rose!" They both shouted. They ran to meet her at the front door before she could even close it behind her.

"Easy, easy, kids. Give me a chance to come in before you jump me."

The kids giggled as they wrapped their arms around her. Addy slid down her leg until he sat on her foot with his arms and legs wrapped around hers. He laughed as she half limped and shuffled along the floor for a few steps with him in tow, seated on her foot.

"Okay, that's it," Rose said. "Get up, guys. We're going to a place where people play dress-up all the time, so they look like old-time princes and princesses. I think it'll be fun for you to see all the silly shows and eat lunch there."

"Come on," I added. "Everyone into the van. The sooner you're in, the quicker we'll get there." I turned to Rose. "By the way, I heard from Sammi. Her mom is sicker than she thought and she's staying on longer as her caregiver until she's better. We'll need to figure out the sitter situation if we're going to keep up with training and other errands."

"I don't like to hear that," Rose said. "It took long enough to do all her background checks as it was."

"You let me know what you want to do. We'll need an alternative we both can live with."

She nodded and headed for the garage. It didn't take long after that to load up the kids with her help. Soon Rose and I were on the road for the Renaissance Faire. I hadn't been to one since I was a teenager and I found myself looking forward to it as much as the kids were, even without the alternative reason she had for going there with us.

I asked Rose, "So are you going to fill me in on why this trip is so important the weekend before school starts?"

"I told you a few weeks ago the kids are old enough to get their protection charms. I had them fashioned and the smith has them ready. The problem is, this weekend he's working at the Ren Faire so we have to go there to pick them up and finish the process of sealing them to the kids."

"What's that entail? Sounds ominous."

Rose waved off my concern with a flick of her wrist. "It's nothing. We have to enact the final magic with the charms worn by them. That's what seals the magic to them. That's all."

"If you say so." I went back to concentrating on my driving. Rose and I shifted to talking about the upcoming start of school. We chatted about school supplies and how Sadie would get to and from school. I had wanted her to ride the bus like a normal kid. However, Rose wanted us to start off driving her to and from school. In the end, I prevailed, and Rose agreed to let Sadie ride the bus with her friends from the neighborhood.

The drive went faster than I expected and before I knew it, we had turned into the grass parking area outside the crenelated wooden fence erected around the faire. I got Addy settled in his stroller while Rose helped Sadie climb out of the van. Rose had purchased our tickets online and we showed the codes from her phone at the gate to get admission.

We spent the first hour just walking around. It was a lot more elaborate than I'd remembered from my youth. Of course, that was close to fifteen years before so I shouldn't be surprised by the changes. We walked and saw some of the sights. I ate a deep-fried turkey leg for lunch. Addy thought that was funny. I even offered him a bite, which he turned down amidst gales of three-year-old laughter.

"I don't like turkey, Unca Chip."

"How do you know?" I asked. "You've never had it before."

He crossed his arms and turned his head away, when I offered a bite one more time. I pulled the offered turkey leg back. I didn't argue with toddlers. I was fine with him eating the chicken fingers and fries I had gotten them from the same booth. Sadie had already gobbled hers down. The kid had a hollow leg sometimes with the way she ate. Rose chalked it up to a heightened Fae metabolism which had to feed both physical and magical growth.

"Come on," Rose said as she stood. "Time to go see the smith. I told him to expect us after our lunch."

"He takes appointments?" I asked.

"For something like this, he does. He knows who our family is. He's connected to the mountain dwarf royal family, and they've long been allies of ours."

"You didn't say he was an Unusual." I wasn't sure what I expected, but it wasn't some sort of dwarf from a Tolkien novel.

"You'll see soon enough. He's not far from here. Come on."

I got Addy back into his stroller to help corral him better. Sadie tagged along in front with Rose. She occasionally pointed to something and asked Rose a question. At one booth they stopped, and Rose bought Sadie a wooden sword to play with as we walked.

I heard the ringing of the smith's hammer before we rounded the corner and saw him for ourselves. My eyes went wide. He actually looked like a dwarf from an epic fantasy tale, though he was taller than I pictured them in stories. He looked more like a short, extremely muscular man with a thick beard and long hair.

He looked up and spotted Rose coming. He put up his tools and whatever he was working on. Then he flipped a sign by the forge from open to closed. The forge had a roof built over it held up by four thick wooden posts. The fire vented through a stone chimney jutting up through the thatched roof. Wooden panels had been attached to two of the four sides to block access to the hot forge and tools inside.

He pulled folding wooden panels across one of the open sides of the forge facing the main thoroughfare and gestured for us to come around to the remaining open side of the forge. He waited at the back of the workshop while we filed in. He held two small leather pouches in his hands and greeted the children with a big grin.

"Your aunt had me make very special presents for you two. Do you want to see them?"

Sadie stopped and looked at me. "Can I?"

"Sure," I said. "That's part of the reason we're here. Be polite and ask nicely, though."

The smith nodded a greeting to me as I spoke. When I finished directing Sadie, I nodded back.

Sadie ran over and held up her hand. "Can I pick which one I want?"

"No, I made one special for each of you. Here, hold out your hand like this." He demonstrated with his palm facing up.

Sadie mimicked him and waited for her reward. The smith opened one of the small pouches and tipped it over until a small gold-and-silver circle about a half inch across spilled out into her palm.

"Oooo, it's so pretty. Look, Aunt Rose. It sparkles." Sadie held up her hand to show us in the shadows of the open room.

I had to agree with her. Even in the shadows beneath the forge's roof, the charm sparkled and twinkled with a light of its own.

I leaned over to Rose. "I see the sparkles. I suppose that'll settle down when she's out in public. I thought we didn't want to draw attention to her?"

"Don't worry, Chip," Rose said. "That's the magic waiting to be bound to her. Once that's done, it will disappear, at least most of the time."

The smith knelt down so he was eye to eye with Sadie. "I want you to take the charm in your fingers and press it up to your forehead." He demonstrated by pressing with his pinched thumb and forefinger against the middle of his head right between his thick, bushy eyebrows.

Sadie smiled and nodded. She picked up the charm from her hand and put it up against her head. As soon as she did, the smith pressed his open hand against her head, holding her hand and the charm in place. He muttered something I couldn't make out. A flash of light escaped around the edges of his hand on Sadie's head.

He pulled his hand down and Sadie took the charm down to look at it. She pouted. "Where are the sparkles? They're gone."

"They're in here," the smith said. He touched the center of her chest with his forefinger. "The magic is in you, along with your own mana. It will forever be there for you to draw upon. Always wear this wherever you go and whatever you do. It will help to keep you safe."

He reached into his pocket and pulled out a delicate gold chain. His thick fingers, calloused and scarred from years in the forge, were surprisingly dexterous. He easily threaded the charm on the thin chain. He leaned forward and attached it around Sadie's neck so the charm hung down against her breast bone. She reached up and touched it.

As she did, a cold flash pressed against my chest as well. I reached up and touched the gold shark's tooth amulet hanging around my own neck. It, too, had magic imparted to me because of spells infused into it by Lili and my brother before their deaths. It was my very special charm. Now Sadie had a charm of her own. Knowing I was still discovering what my shark's tooth could do, I wondered what her charm did.

"What will it do?" I asked. "I don't want her to surprise us with anything out in public by accident."

The smith nodded at Rose. "At the request of the Princess, I infused it with copper and silver to give her agility of mind and body. It also has a core of cold iron to resist evil spells directed at her. It won't give complete protection but will blunt the effects some."

The smith stood and moved over to Addy. He knelt down and held a similar charm up to the toddler's forehead. Once again he spoke words of power I didn't understand. After he sealed the power in Addy's charm, he strung it on a short leather thong and tied it around the boy's neck to dangle onto his chest, too.

"His charm imparts strength of character and physique through titanium and platinum as he is destined to become his sister's weapons master. There is also a similar core of cold iron for protection."

Rose said, "Thank you for your service to our family. We will not forget what you have done for us here." She stopped for a second and glanced my way before saying, "Have you given further consideration to my other request?"

The smith looked my way, then back to Rose. "I have not yet reached a decision."

Rose let the matter drop and said, "Well, we don't want to keep you from your fans here at the faire any longer. Thank you again for the charms."

She took the stroller and pushed it out of the forge area and back onto the main path through the Ren Faire. I took Sadie by the hand and rushed to catch up with her.

As soon as I caught up, I asked, "Would you like to explain that last little interchange between you and the dwarf?"

"It is nothing. He has a decision to make and until he does, there is nothing to discuss. Let's go back to the car. Addy's going to get cranky soon and want to nap in the car on the way home."

She brushed me off and moved towards the exit and the parking lot, pushing Addy in his stroller. I followed with Sadie in tow. I had a feeling I was missing something important.

# Rose

The alarm went off and I groaned. It was bright and early on the first day of school. Placing wards around Sadie's elementary school had kept me up well into the wee hours of the morning. I reached out for my nightstand to tap snooze on my phone. I could sleep a little longer.

Then I saw the time. Clearly, I'd tapped the snooze too many times already. I was going to be late for Sadie's first day of school if I didn't get moving in a hurry. I sat up, rubbing the sleep from my eyes in an attempt to wake up faster. With no time for a shower to help shock me awake, I opted to stumble out and pick up a giant chilled latte from the donut place on the way to see Chip and the kids.

I pulled my hair back, trying to gather the unruly waves that resisted containment in something as confining as a ponytail. I wrestled the errant strands into position after a few aggravating seconds. The elastic band looped around my wrist served to tame my morning do so I could show my face in public.

The drive-thru line took way too long, but at least I didn't spill the large plastic cup full of iced coffee into my lap. I gunned the Firebird's engine and pulled out into traffic. I was going to be too late to have breakfast, but if I hurried I could still get there before her bus picked up at her stop.

My excitement for Sadie had an undertone of sadness that she was growing up so fast. It didn't seem all that long ago that I met her for the first time at the hospital. Lili had held out her firstborn child for me to cradle in my arms, telling me the name she and Bobby had chosen. I remember looking down into those deep blue eyes that captivated me in an instant and I'd nodded my head in a slight bow to my future queen.

Now she was a big girl first grader and going to school for the first time, and I was going to miss it all if I didn't hurry. I reminded myself to ease up on the accelerator despite my sense of urgency. It was the first day of school and there were lots of kids standing near the streets of the development.

I pulled into the driveway next to Chip's minivan and hopped out to race to the door. It opened before I could get there.

"Aunt Rose, you're late." Sadie crossed her arms and pushed out her lower lip in a pout. "We were supposed to have breakfast with you today."

"I know sweetie. The morning got away from me. But I'm here in time for you to get on the bus."

Chip came over to the door with Addy running behind him. "Turn around, Rose. We're on the way out, not in. It's time to go to the bus stop."

"I'm glad I made it in time for that at least. Sorry, Chip. I know I promised to be here."

"We can talk later. Let's go or we'll miss the bus."

I stepped back to make room for Chip and the two kids to exit the front door. "You know there's still time to decide to homeschool her."

"No, we discussed this. I let you talk me into it last year for kindergarten and I've regretted the decision. She needs to meet and play with kids her own age."

"There are the neighborhood kids. We've vetted them at least."

Chip didn't answer right away. He took Addy by the hand. "Sadie, sweetie, hold your aunt's hand while we walk to the bus stop." He started down the sidewalk to the street and turned towards the corner at the end of the cul-de-sac. A group of parents and kids had already assembled there ahead of us.

"Lili and Bobby wanted Sadie to have a normal life growing up. You know that. That includes going to school with the other kids. It'll be good for her."

"I want to go to school, Aunt Rose," Sadie added. "All my friends go to school, and they tell me how much fun it is. I can't wait to do that, too."

"I know." I did know. I remembered my days in school. But things were different then and I didn't have a target on my head as the future of Fae royalty.

Ellie Johnson, the short redhead from across the street, stepped out from a crowd of moms and waved to Chip and me. "Hurry up. There's still time to get Sadie in a picture with the rest of the kids for the first day photo."

Chip smiled. "I'm glad you keep up with the protocol on these things, Ellie. I'm hopeless when it comes to that stuff."

She nudged me with her elbow and grinned back at him. "Don't worry, Chip. I've got your back. Besides, you've settled in perfectly these last two years. You're an old hand at this stuff by now."

Ellie reached out and directed Sadie to stand in a line with the ten other kids of various ages waiting at the bus stop for the elementary school bus. Sadie fell in with the other kids, her backpack over her shoulders looking way too big for her tiny frame. I blinked away a few tears as my eyes welled up. I couldn't help but think of Lili at times like this. She would have been so proud of her little girl. Chip was right. This was what Lili wanted, even knowing the potential risks.

I pulled out my phone and knelt to snap a few photos of the group and then zoomed in to crop out the others so I just had Sadie in the frame. That was when I saw the dark sedan parked down the street. Something about it didn't seem right to me and I stopped taking the picture and looked up past the line of kids to stare at it with my naked eyes and not through my phone's camera lens.

The windows of the sedan were heavily tinted, and I couldn't make out the driver behind the wheel or tell if there was anyone else in the vehicle besides the shadowy form in the driver's seat. I realized what had caught my eye as I studied the car a little longer. Its engine was running. It was also pulled over in front of an empty stretch of grass and not in front of any of the homes in particular.

I stood and kept my gaze on the car as the bus finally drove up. I missed Sadie climbing aboard and tore my eyes away long enough to wave at her through the windows on the side of the bus as it pulled away.

"Rose," Chip said, breaking through my thoughts. "What's got you so distracted? I asked if you could send me the pictures you took. I left my phone in the kitchen at home."

"Uh, yeah, sure." I hooked a thumb over my shoulder. "That sedan over there, have you seen it before?"

Chip looked around and shrugged. "What sedan?"

I whipped around and stared at the empty stretch of street. The bus had obscured it when it drove off, so I hadn't seen the car pull away from where it was parked. "I need to go, Chip. I'll send you the pictures." I ran back down the sidewalk to the house.

Behind me, Ellie said. "She's off in a hurry."

Chip said. "Yeah, she's like that sometimes."

I didn't hear the rest of the conversation. My heart pounded with a sensation that something was wrong. I needed to go after that car and see where it went. I made it to my car and jumped in, racing back out of the cul-de-sac past all the parents and smaller children still standing at the bus stop. A few frowned at my speed. I didn't care. I had to find that car.

It turned out, I didn't have to hurry all that much. I caught up less than a minute later. The car had pulled over a hundred yards behind the bus as it stopped to pick up more kids. I wondered if he was just stuck behind the school bus as it made its stops or if the person inside followed the bus itself.

I pulled behind a car down the street and studied the sedan. The window was down, and a large telephoto lens poked out for a few seconds aimed at the bus and the kids boarding. Had they photographed Sadie and the other kids, too?

I gripped the wheel in a white-knuckled squeeze. There was no way I could go over there and do anything no matter what my feelings were. Taking pictures of kids at a bus stop was creepy but not inherently illegal or worthy of my intervention. I needed to know more.

The bus pulled away and so did the car, taking its time not to get too close to the bus. I held back until they reached the corner leading out to the main road outside the neighborhood. As soon as the sedan turned after the bus, I pulled out and zoomed down to the intersection to follow both vehicles.

The sedan followed the bus all the way to the school, pulling off beside the playing fields near the school with a clear view of the buses unloading kids out front. I drove past, trying to catch a glimpse of the driver as I went by. The tinted windows foiled my attempt to identify anyone. I went by the school and drove to the next intersection. A small strip mall was across the street, so I waited at the light, staring at the parked sedan in my rearview mirror so I didn't lose sight of it.

When the light changed, I crossed over the road and into the shopping center lot. I did a quick loop through the parking area and returned to the light that would take me back past the school. The sedan had moved and was now at the intersection across from me with its left turn blinker on. I prayed he got the light first so I could follow him.

I got lucky and he pulled out into the intersection and passed to the left across in front of me. I immediately put on my right blinker and checked the traffic before pulling out to go after them. I didn't care if they spotted me at this point. I planned on confronting them to see what they were up to. I tapped the phone open as I drove, hitting a number in my favorites list. Warren picked up on the third ring.

"Yeah, Rose?"

"Hey, you still have that friend in the Sheriff's office?"

"I do. Why?" He didn't sound too irritated at the question.

"I need you to run a plate for me. I'm trailing them now. They were following Sadie's bus and taking pics of the kids at other stops."

"That's creepy. Give me the tag number."

I read off the plate of the car in front of me. "Did you get that?"

The sedan had picked up speed and changed lanes to go around the traffic in front of him on the dual lane road we were on.

"I got it," Warren replied. "Am I doing this as a favor, or do you plan on paying me for the information?"

"This guy's a probable pedophile and you want to get paid for uncovering them?"

"Jeeze, Rose. When you say it that way, it makes me sound bad." Warren could be so touchy sometimes.

"Just track down the owner and call me back. I need to follow this guy and see where they're going."

I hung up and swerved into the next lane to catch up to them. They'd gotten several cars ahead of me into an open stretch of road and accelerated for the next intersection while it was still green. Right before they got to the traffic light, the driver reached a hand out the window and pointed at the lights. The unmistakable glow of magic burst from the outstretched hand and enveloped the light. The lights went amber and then turned red just as they passed underneath them.

The cars ahead of me slowed and I banged both hands on the steering wheel as the cars around me blocked me from following after the person. The use of magic clinched my suspicions, though. They were not just a random creeper searching for their next target. This had to have something to do with Sadie and that meant that someone else had tracked her down to figure out her true identity.

Cursing to myself while I waited at the light, I knew I had at least gotten the license plate number. Warren would get that back to me and I could track down the person by the end of the day. At the very least I'd know who they were.

The light finally changed to green, and I waited my turn to head through the intersection. I planned on trying to get ahead of the pack of cars in front of me and continue on in an attempt to catch up, but I didn't have much hope. I'd been made and the sedan was probably long gone by now. I'd just have to wait for Warren to call back.

# 5

# Chip

Sadie's first week of school went by quickly. Based on the work coming home, I realized they were still assessing Sadie's abilities. She'd entered first grade a confident reader already. She'd been reading since she was four. The assignments they sent home with her weren't much of a challenge to her, but we had fun completing them anyway. It was an enjoyable time together every day after she got off the bus. I had coloring pages and other activities for Addy to do while Sadie and I looked at her little bit of homework each day. Mostly it was a single sheet of simple word and letter matching or some basic arithmetic exercises. It never took us long.

I had stopped at the library on my regular rounds to get some recommended books for young kids and we picked one from the pile to read a chapter together every day. Addy settled in to listen when I read out loud even though there were no pictures to see. The current book was about a kid who had discovered a mystery in her school that needed solving. Sadie became instantly invested and wanted me to read ahead. I told her if she wanted to do that, she'd have to do it herself since I had to do some housework.

To my surprise, after I'd said that for the third or fourth time, she picked up the book after I got up from the sofa and settled it in her lap to keep reading. I smiled and led Addy away to go outside and play in the back yard. My mother had done something similar to me when I was about that age. It had instilled in me a lifelong love of reading and stories. I hoped it would do the same for her.

Sadie still sat reading when I came in from playing with Addy to make dinner. I had hoped I could get her to keep her brother occupied while I cooked, but I could see she was enthralled with her story. Instead, I brought Addy with me into the kitchen and settled him on a chair to watch a few kid videos on my phone while I started gathering ingredients for our meal.

I was halfway through cutting up the veggies before I roasted them in the oven when Sadie called out from the other room. "Uncle Chip, there's a fox man in the back yard."

That stopped me. I walked over to look out through the window in the back door, parting the curtain with the eight-inch chef's knife I still had in my hand.

What I saw froze me in place for a split second. A person in a green hoodie was hunched over peering through the back sliding door right outside where Sadie sat reading. It wasn't a fox, but it was a man.

I broke through my shock and pulled open the back door. My feet propelled me forward with my knife in hand and I shouted at the intruder.

"Get the hell away from there!"

The person turned to face me; his eyes wide as he backpedaled away from the angry homeowner with a knife charging at him.

I held the knife close and reached out with my free hand to grab at the man's arm. He whipped it out of the way, moving almost faster than I expected.

He spun around on one foot and kicked out with the other at my knife hand.

I barely avoided the kick and its attempt to disarm me. I remembered my training with Rose and instantly lunged forward, trying to take advantage of his extension with the kick.

To my surprise, he once again moved so quickly he seemed to blur for a second. When his form solidified again, he stood inside my reach and chopped down with the edge of his hand at my wrist.

Pain lanced through my forearm and my fingers went numb. The knife dropped to the ground.

In desperation, I pressed outward with my free hand, palm outward. I drew upon my Guardian ability to create a barrier, only this time I focused it all into a smaller area in front of me in a flat plane about two feet square. Then I pushed with all my mental strength.

The guy's eyes widened, and he flew backward to crash into the wooden castle swing set in the back yard.

I didn't hesitate. Rose had said never to slow down or give up until I knew my adversary was out of the fight. I ran forward, scooping up the knife again in my tingling fingers and leveled the blade under the man's chin so the sharp chef's blade lay against his neck.

"Don't you dare move, you asshole."

The man stared up at me and spread his hands wide at his side. He sat on the grass with blood trickling down from his nose and the corner of his mouth.

"I won't hurt you," he said. "I was just searching for something, and it led me to this home."

"You'll have to do better than that," I said. "I'm calling the police."

"No, don't. I don't mean you any harm. I was tracking someone else and didn't understand why there were so many wards guarding this home. I wondered what was hidden in this simple suburban house. That's all."

"You can see the wards? They're supposed to be invisible." I knew he wasn't human because of his crazy fast speed. I didn't know that meant he could also see the protections on the house. I needed to tell Rose how he saw what he saw. Being able to see the protections kind of defeated the purpose of hiding behind them.

"I'm a Kitsune. Some of us can learn to see magical protections. What kind of Unusual are you? You smell human, but I've never seen a human do anything like what you just did."

"I'm special. That's all you need to know." Something he said earlier came back to me. "You said you were tracking someone. Who is it you're after?" I wanted to find out if he was looking for Sadie.

His eyes shot from side to side like a trapped animal before he answered. "You're just going to kill me anyway, so why should I answer you?"

That caught me by surprise. "I don't want to kill you. You're the one who came snooping around my house and spying on my niece. That's why I came after you." I lowered my knife but brought my other hand up ready to push him down with my barrier if he tried to do anything.

The answer seemed to placate him a little. "I'm looking for a hunter, one who killed my fiancée last year. I've been looking ever since she died. The trail brought me here to this neighborhood and the corner down the street from here. When I saw the home with all the protections, I assumed it was linked somehow." He looked down at his hands. They trembled until he clenched them for a second. "I guess I was wrong about that. I'm sorry. The hunter I was after must have just driven by this place."

Now my radar was up. I knew Rose had been trying to find out who it was that trailed the bus to school that first day. Did that have something to do with what this guy was looking for? I didn't believe in coincidences, just lucky chances that gave opportunities if you were prepared to take advantage of them. Maybe these two things were linked.

"I'm Chip. I live here with my niece and nephew. The protections on the house are there because I'm human and the kids aren't, as you already know."

"You're not human, at least not completely. You have magic of your own. I felt it come from you when you cast that force spell on me."

"Look, what's your name? Let's start there."

"I'm Godo."

"Hi, Godo. If I step back, will you run away? I promise, I would like to know who you're following, too. It might have something to do with my family as well."

"How? I clearly stumbled upon you all by accident."

I laughed. "Maybe, and then again, maybe not. Let me call someone to come and meet with us. She might be able to help you with your search and she's a better person to understand why our wards were visible to you in the first place."

"As long as she doesn't attack me like you did."

"Like I said, it was only because you were trespassing. Come over to the picnic table. I'll get you an ice pack for your face. I need to go inside and check on the kids anyway."

I reached down and offered him help getting up. After I pulled him to his feet, we moved over so he could sit on the bench beside the picnic table.

"Look, I'll be right back. I have to get my phone and I need to make sure they're okay inside. Don't run away. I think we can help each other out here if you'll be patient."

Godo frowned and put a hand to his head. "I don't feel much like running right now. I'll stay. Don't forget that ice pack. I'll also take some painkillers if you have any. Your magic hits like a concrete slab in the face."

"I'll be right back." I walked back inside and shut the back door behind me before I let the realization of the whole incident hit me. I had a momentary bout with some tremors of my own as the adrenaline drained from my system. Then I went into the kitchen. Addy hadn't even moved from where he watched videos on my phone. I peeked into the family room. Sadie stood with her nose pressed against the back sliding door.

"Sadie, come away from there."

"Hey, Uncle Chip. Why did you beat up the fox man?"

"Why do you keep calling him that?" I didn't understand her meaning.

"That's what he looks like. I can see a fox inside him, wanting to come out."

"Come here and play with your brother for a second. I need to call Aunt Rose." I picked up my phone, ignoring Addy's groan of protest. I searched for Kitsune in my browser and immediately found an entry for a fox shifter of Japanese origin. So, Sadie was right. He was a fox man after all.

"Addy, go and play with Sadie. I need my phone for a little bit."

Sadie held out her hand. "Come on. We can play with your blocks and build towers."

"Knock down?" he asked, indicating his favorite part of tower building.

"Sure. Come on." Sadie led him from the room.

I dialed Rose and waited for her to pick up.

"What is it, Chip? I'm busy with something."

"Are you around town? I had a situation here at the house."

"What kind of situation?" She asked. "I didn't feel any of the wards trip."

"That's part of the problem. I'll explain it all when you get here."

"I need more than that, Chip. I'm trying to track down that guy from the first day of school."

"Good, because I think I have a lead. A Kitsune showed up at the house and I think he might have some answers for you."

"A what?" The urgency changed in her voice right away. "Are the kids okay? He didn't hurt anyone, did he?"

"No, he's sitting out back right now waiting for me to come back. I think you need to talk to him, too. I'll wait until you get here to ask him any more questions. He needs some medical attention after I jumped him in the back yard."

"You jumped him?" Rose didn't sound convinced of my description.

"You can ask him yourself when you get here. See you soon." I hung up the call because I didn't feel like listening to her disparage my fighting abilities right after I'd won a fight against a supernatural opponent.

I checked on the kids in the family room playing blocks and then grabbed a bag of frozen peas from the freezer and headed out to the backyard. Godo sat on the bench where I left him. He still had a bit of the trapped animal gaze in his eyes. I tried to move in slow, easy movements as I walked over to him.

"Here, put this on your face where it hurts. It'll help a little." I knew since he was a shifter, he probably had some regenerative abilities but that didn't mean his injuries didn't hurt.

"Ahhhh," he said when he pressed the frozen peas to his face. "That feels good."

"I called my sister-in-law. She's coming to meet you. She might have some information about the person you're chasing."

"Is that the little girl's mother? You said you're the uncle."

"She's their aunt. It's complicated. We both take care of the kids now." I needed to change the subject. Curious about what drove him to come here after his fiancée's killer, I went in that direction. "Your dead fiancée, tell me about her. Was she a Kitsune, too?"

"No, she was a member of the Fae nobility living in California. Her family comes originally from Japan, like me."

That caught me by surprise. He didn't look Asian, though I'd learned from my search that was where Kitsune came from originally.

"You're from Japan?"

"I'm only one-eighth Japanese on my mother's side. That's where my power comes from. My great-grandmother was a powerful Kitsune who lived in America when World War II broke out. She and others like her were imprisoned because they feared our kind would side with the Emperor against America, even though we were American citizens. Eventually, the war ended, and she was released. Her family had lost everything, their businesses and homes, so she drifted around the country from job to job until she settled again in Northern California. That was where she met a lumberjack who wasn't afraid of what she really was. They settled down and started a family and three generations later, here I am."

"It wasn't one of our greatest moments in American history. I'm sorry people are such scared assholes when things get stressful."

"Like you said, I don't even look Japanese so it doesn't affect me all that much, but I wish it hadn't been that way. She never talked about the camps much, but it must have been horrible."

I realized we'd gotten off track and shifted the conversation back to his fiancée. "But your girlfriend was Japanese Fae nobility?"

"Yes. That was why the hunter must have come after her. There were clues he left that he was searching for something to do with Fae nobility. As soon as he killed her, he left the area, and it took me a very long time to track him all the way to the east coast. He's left a trail of dead Fae women in his wake. All of them were associated with some Fae noble or royal lines in some way."

That perked up my radar. If this hunter was tracking down Fae nobles and royals, he could be homing in on Sadie, Addy, or maybe even Rose. That was something we needed to find out as soon as possible. I checked the time on my phone. I needed Rose to get here sooner than later. This definitely fell into her side of our partnership in taking care of the kids. I settled in to wait and asked Godo about his dead fiancée to pass the time.

## 6

## Rose

I didn't bother going inside the house when I got to the neighborhood. Chip had said the Kitsune was out back. I held my enchanted silver sword down close by my side as I walked quickly around the house. It wouldn't do for the neighbors to wonder why Aunt Rose was running around with a shiny and very real sword at dinner time.

I reached out and unlatched the gate to let myself inside the tall fence surrounding the backyard. I let the sword swing free to be ready. The wooden fence would hide any fighting that happened. I didn't know who this fox shifter was, but they didn't belong in my niece and nephew's yard.

Chip and a stranger sat across from each other at the picnic table. He didn't look like any Kitsune I'd ever met, primarily because he didn't look Japanese. I knew they weren't all Japanese, but that was the norm. The guy also looked like a board had smacked him in the face. He had two rapidly developing black eyes. I wondered if Chip had done that. If he had, I would have to give him kudos. Kitsune were tough fighters in most situations. They were known to be fast and crafty.

The two of them noticed me coming their way. The Kitsune's eyes shifted immediately to my bare blade. He stood and took up a fighting stance.

"I thought you said you two wouldn't hurt me," he shouted at Chip.

Chip swung around and pointed at my sword. "Whoa, whoa, hold on everybody. There's been a misunderstanding here. Rose, put the sword away. You don't need it. Godo isn't a threat."

"How do you know?" I asked.

"He's chasing a person who's been killing Fae all across the country. His search led him here to Westminster."

I hadn't heard about any notable and unexplained Fae deaths, but I hadn't been plugged into my usual network lately like I had in the past.

I lowered my sword. "Okay, Chip. Start at the beginning and don't leave anything out."

Godo didn't return to his seat. He still eyed my bared blade. But he didn't run either. Chip explained what had happened and what he'd learned.

When he finished, I said, "And you think he's after the same guy I am after? That's good, Chip. If someone is tracking and killing Fae nobility, they might be here for the same thing."

Godo said, "You don't need to worry about the children or Chip. None of the other victims were children or men. All were adult women as far as I know."

I was glad to hear that, but it still might be someone searching for links to the next Fae queen. That put Sadie in danger.

"Can you describe this person?"

Godo shrugged. "I don't know much. I'm pretty sure it's a man, primarily because I tracked them back to hunter clan magic based on some mana residue I found on the scene of one of the murders."

"What kind of residue?" I asked.

"I'm sensitive to magic spells of certain sorts, as I told you. I was able to piece together the left-over power of a basic protection spell that might exist on a charm or talisman. The hunters use things like that since they don't have magic of their own."

"It could have been from the victim," Chip offered. "How do you know it was from the hunter?"

Godo thought about the question for a few seconds then said, "The spell had a, uh, sort of masculine flavor to it. That's the only way I could describe it. I just assumed since the victim was a female that it came from the attacker."

He was probably right. It also meant that he might be able to sense this magic again if the hunter was close. That could be helpful if I was going to track this Fae hunter down and deal with him.

I looked around and asked, "Chip, where are the kids? Have you checked on them?"

"Yes, They're safe inside. Sadie is playing with Addy in the family room. I was making dinner when Sadie spotted him. She called him the fox man."

I glanced at Godo. "You shifted form here in the open?"

"No, I looked like I do now. I don't know how she saw through my human self to see the Kitusne inside."

That was another thing we needed to figure out. If Sadie could see the true selves of Unusuals, that would be a rare and valuable talent. It was also something we needed to teach her about. She couldn't go around outing people's secret identities in public. Chip and I would have to deal with that, too, now.

"Let's go inside and talk some more," I said. "The kids shouldn't be left alone, and Chip needs to keep making dinner. I hope there's enough for all of us."

Chip rolled his eyes. "I can stretch what I had planned to feed us all. Godo, come on in. I'll make sure Rose puts the sword away. She knows she doesn't need it now."

He was mostly correct. I was also reasonably sure Godo wasn't a threat, but I didn't want to put the sword back in the Firebird yet. I'd keep it close by just in case.

I started to the back door. "You two can work on dinner. I'll go and play with the kids. I want to talk with Sadie about what she saw."

Chip and Godo followed me inside. The beginnings of some chopped veggies were out on the island counter. I didn't know what else he had planned, but I was sure there'd be plenty to eat. Chip always made enough to have leftovers the next day. I pushed through the swinging door into the dining room and the open family room beyond. Sadie and Addy sat playing just as Chip had said. That all ended when Addy spotted me.

"Aunt Rose!" He jumped up and ran over as fast as his little legs could carry him.

I scooped him up into my arms, leaning in to blow raspberries against his arm. He giggled and wriggled in my grasp. I hugged him close and then set him down. Sadie came over and hugged me tight around the waist.

"Aunt Rose, Uncle Chip fought with the fox man out back. Did he tell you about what happened?"

"What did you see exactly?" I wanted to know more about how she'd uncovered Godo's Unusual type without him showing some outward sign.

"I was sitting reading my book when I felt like I was being watched. I turned and saw the fox man looking in at me through the back sliding door. I called out to Uncle Chip, and he went out and fought him. Then they stopped and started talking. I was glad. I didn't want either of them to get hurt."

"Me either, honey. Tell me more about what you saw that told you he was a fox underneath the human form he wore?"

Sadie laughed. "I don't know. Sometimes I see others who have a hidden inside self. I stopped telling you and Uncle Chip when I was younger. You didn't see what I saw and didn't believe me."

"I'm sorry. We should have paid more attention to what you were saying. What about a person like that do you see exactly?"

"It's sort of like there's a type of themselves that's right there behind them. If I look hard enough, I can separate the two and see them for what the hidden part is. Was I right? Is the guy from outside a fox shifter?"

"He is," I said. "He didn't mean to scare you and Uncle Chip. He was here looking for a bad person he'd followed through here and thought they might live here. He was wrong and he knows that now."

"That's good." She cocked her head to the side. "I hear someone in the kitchen with Uncle Chip. Is the fox man staying for dinner?"

"He is."

She clapped her hands together. "Do you think he'll show his fox self to us? I want to see it."

"That's a rude thing to ask someone, Sadie. It is personal to him and many like him don't want to share that part of themselves with others."

"Oh," Sadie said. She cast her eyes down, chastised.

I reached out and lifted up her chin. "You didn't know. That's why I told you. It's okay, just remember that in the future, okay?"

She nodded. "Okay. When's dinner?"

I laughed. There was my normal Sadie. Her appetite right now was bottomless. She must be in a growth spurt. She was getting so big so fast.

"You were reading a book, you said? Why don't you sit down on the sofa and tell me about it while I play blocks with Addy. Dinner will be ready as soon as Uncle Chip can finish it."

At the mention of her book, Sadie's eyes brightened. She ran to the sofa and picked up a chapter book. That surprised me and made me proud of her at the same time.

"Oh, Aunt Rose, I can't wait to tell you about this one. It's so good." She sat down while I climbed down to the floor with Addy to build towers so he could knock them down. The whole time I played with her brother, Sadie explained the entire story to me in great detail. I savored the sort of normal moment in time for what it was. Times like this were fleeting in life, especially when there was danger everywhere I looked in the outside world. In my line of work, I'd seen too often how quickly life could be ripped away from what you always knew as normal.

Sadie and Addy had been so young when their parents died. That was a good thing in a way. They had quickly settled into their new normal with Chip, and I was able to lend to the stability in their lives whenever I was around to watch over them. It wasn't perfect, but the kids seemed to thrive in spite of that.

Chip poked his head in from the kitchen. "Dinner's ready. Can you get the kids cleaned up? I've set up the round table here in the kitchen to eat, if that's okay?"

"Fine by me." I stood. "You heard Uncle Chip. Let's go and wash those grubby hands and go eat dinner." I sniffed at the air and the deliciousness wafting in from the kitchen. "It smells extra yummy. If you don't hurry, I'm going to beat you all to the food."

The kids giggled and leaped to their feet, racing to the powder room down the hallway by the stairs to wash up. I laughed and walked along behind them. It didn't take the three of us long to wash our hands and go to the kitchen. Godo sat at the table with his back to the corner. Sadie and Addy stopped as soon as they saw the stranger.

"Kids," Chip said. "This is Mr. Godo. He's having dinner with us. He's also sorry about frightening everyone when he was in the backyard." Chip stared at the visitor, waiting for a response.

"Uh, yeah, I'm sorry I scared you all. I was looking for someone and they weren't here like I thought they were."

"Uncle Chip fought you. I saw it all." Sadie beamed at her uncle then looked at Godo. "Did he hurt you? I saw you fall against the castle."

"I'm fine now. Your Uncle and I figured out the mistake before anyone was hurt badly."

Chip added, "It's a good lesson about not jumping to conclusions about people just because they look or act differently from you. Do you understand that?"

"Yes, Uncle Chip." Sadie took her seat at the table and settled behind her plate.

I picked up Addy and placed him in his booster seat so he could sit high enough to use the table, too. Chip carried a large platter over with pieces of roasted chicken and vegetables. There were potatoes, carrots, green beans, and Brussels sprouts spread around the chicken. The dinner looked amazing, and I realized it had been a while since I'd come over for a home-cooked meal. My single lifestyle had me eating carryout and whatever I could scrounge around my apartment.

I savored the food and company, but I kept a watchful eye on Godo. He was a stranger in this home and until I knew him better and had a chance to check up on his backstory, I would consider him as a potential threat. Warren could probably get a handle on whether he was telling the truth or not. I decided to call the werewolf investigator as soon as I left this evening. While I was here, though, I'd learn what I could so I'd have information to pass along to speed up the search.

# 7

# Chip

The Kitsune left with Rose as soon as dinner was finished. He'd promised to show her all the evidence he'd gathered while chasing after the hunter. He kept it all in his car, which was parked in a nearby cul-de-sac. She'd agreed to follow him back to it. After they were gone, I realized I was glad to see him leave. I hadn't realized how tense I was when he was in the house with us. While he might be a valuable source of information on who the mysterious bus tracker was, he had made the bad decision to creep around and lurk in our backyard uninvited. He might be useful to us, but that didn't give him a total pass.

Godo was the only one who had any idea who our adversary might be. If it was the same person who'd tracked the bus on the first day of school they'd killed more than once already, and it wasn't a leap to think they were here to kill again. Just thinking about the possible risk to Sadie made fear for her well up inside me. Rose had insisted she had it under control, even though she'd been unable to track the license plate number down from her earlier chase. The plate had been stolen from another vehicle. Godo said that was something the hunter had done in previous crimes, too.

I pushed aside the thoughts about the possibility of the hunter being close by and focused instead on getting the kids ready for bed.

The familiarity of settling down into the normal routine eased my mind from obsessing about risks to the kids. It was bath night. Sadie went first and I left her alone to tend to herself after I drew the bath for her. She was a big girl now and needed her privacy. That gave me time to get Addy ready for his turn. We read a few of his books until his sister was finished in the bathroom. Then I went in and gave Addy his bath and got him dressed for bed.

After I got him settled, I said good night to Brunna, his bed troll, and pulled the door closed. She'd manifested soon after his first birthday. When she arrived, she said something about a child being able to form and understand language that signaled the onset of more intense dreams for a Fae child. Though a female bed troll, Brunna looked a lot like Bernard, just a little less hairy around the face.

Sadie sat on her bed. A large, leather-bound book lay open on her lap. She flipped through the thick parchment pages, looking at the illuminated text and images inside. The ornate illustrations beside the hand-written text seemed to vibrate when I glanced at the pages. Then I saw some of the figures in the images shift position or turn their heads.

Alarmed, I said, "Sadie, should you be looking at that? It looks like it's magical in nature."

"It is, Uncle Chip. I'm okay. It's a book of family lore and history. Aunt Allura gave it to me a few months ago while you were at one of your training sessions with Aunt Rose. She said it was important for me to start learning about the family." She flipped forward towards the last few pages in the book. "Look, Addy and I are in here, along with a description of Mommy and Daddy and our family."

I half-sat on the edge of the bed and leaned over so I could see better. There was a whole page for Sadie and the rest of her family. Each name linked to others by branches in a stylized family tree drawn on the page. Lili and Bobby each had a red "deceased" written below their names. At the bottom of the page, a separate branch of the tree arched off from Bobby and my name appeared on the page. Beneath my name was the title "Guardian."

"Look, Uncle Chip. The whole thing is magically interactive. Touch one of the names."

I extended my finger and touched Bobby's entry. A box appeared to hover over the page.

*Robert Proctor died during an attack on the family by factions unknown. Avenged by Princess Rose Eldersdottir and Charles Henderson Proctor, Guardian.*

IT WAS PARTIALLY CORRECT. We'd tracked down those immediately responsible for their deaths, but Rose and I both believed someone else had been behind that attack and the ones on Sadie later in the forest.

"That's very interesting, Sadie. I'm glad you have something like this connecting you back to your family. It's important that you understand your roots."

"It shows all sorts of things that happened to family members in the past, even long ago. It's like a real-life fairy tale."

I nodded and laid my hand on top of Sadie's head. "You can read for a little while if you want, but don't stay up too late. You have school in the morning."

She was a good reader, so I didn't worry about her being in over her head in the family history tome. I wondered if I should read it, too. Maybe I'd gain some insights into dealing with my in-laws, like Rose. I filed that idea away for a day when I was home and Sadie was at school. Maybe there were stories in there that Addy would enjoy learning about, too.

With the kids asleep for the night, I decided to lock up and get a good night's sleep of my own. The fight with Godo earlier had drawn upon some of my Guardian energy. A good night's sleep would go a long way to restoring my mana stores. While I thought about my earlier fight in the back yard, I remembered how I'd used my Guardian barrier magic to hurl Godo across the yard. It was the first time I'd tried to use it as more than just a defensive spell. That made me wonder if I could hone my control over the barrier and use it in other ways. It had first manifested as a broad, transparent wall of force, but with Godo, I'd focused it into a small square area and pushed at the Kitsune with my will. How focused could I make the powerful force?

Intrigued, I went to the kitchen and flicked on the back lights. My thoughts of sleep had been banished by the questions whirling through my head. I rummaged in the recycling bin until I recovered six rinsed-out cans from dinner a few nights before. I had something I wanted to try.

Outside, I lined the cans up on the edge of the picnic table and then walked around the table to stand by the bench on the opposite side. I was only about six feet away from the cans. Reaching out with my right hand, I extended my forefinger and pointed at the can on the left.

I drew upon my Guardian energy and put the barrier at the end of my finger. I concentrated on it and envisioned it narrowing down until it was a horizontal cylinder like an invisible arrow. The cans beckoned to me from beyond my reach and I stared at the left-hand can while I pushed as hard as I could with the narrow arrow of force.

A flash of sparks and light momentarily blinded me. I blinked away the spots in front of my eyes and smiled. The can on the left wasn't there anymore. I walked around the table to look for the can. Instead of an intact can that was knocked from the table, I found a jagged, twisted and curved piece of steel. It looked like the whole can was there, but it had been blasted apart from the inside out as if my arrow of force had pierced the side of the can and then expanded inside the can with enough force to rip it open. That scared me and I wondered if there was a way to refine the level of force I used. I was going to need more cans.

An hour and a half later, I'd come close to figuring it out. I'd also used up every empty can and plastic container from my recycling bin in the garage. I'd made a huge mess around the picnic table, but I'd managed to refine my power so I did not destroy the last few containers I'd knocked from the side of the picnic table.

I wiped at the sweat dripping from my head. I was drained. The mana pool inside me had dried up with the last trickle of force I'd used on the final empty milk jug. All I wanted to do now was to go inside and sleep, but I couldn't leave the back yard looking like someone had emptied their garbage out there.

I pulled out the rolling recycling bin from the garage and dragged it behind me while I bent down and put all the destroyed metal and plastic parts back inside. It took almost fifteen minutes before I was reasonably sure I'd gotten the worst of the debris. I'd have to check again in the morning when the sun lit up the back yard better. With the recycling bin standing by the back door, I went inside and locked up the house for the night. My bed called to me in my magically drained stupor. I stumbled up the steps and fell onto the mattress, where I crawled up to lay my head on the pillow. Sleep took me the second I closed my eyes.

## 8

# Rose

Godo was a wealth of information. Warren and I had worked through all the leads we had come up with when we combined our information with what he'd amassed during his nationwide manhunt. It had taken the better part of a week to do so, and we were no closer to identifying the hunter Godo chased. We also had no luck determining if that person was the same one I had seen trailing the school bus that first day of school. There were things that linked the two cases but only minor circumstantial evidence. There was nothing concrete.

The Kitsune and Warren had figured out that all of the Fae killed, including Godo's fiancée, had been Fae nobles who were loosely related to Sadie. Most of the links had to be tracked back many generations to find, but they were there. I was sure that made Sadie the next target. I said as much to him while we sat outside the elementary school one evening after it had gotten dark.

Warren wasn't convinced. "Rose, you have to admit there are at least thirty other Fae in the state of Maryland that are also distantly related to the dead nobles."

"None of them are the future Fae queen, Warren. That always makes her the primary target in my book. We need to dig deeper and find this guy."

"That's why we're here. The Parent Teacher Association meeting tonight is under the hunter's moon. Godo said this was when he'd calculated the next attack would happen. He's probably right. That moon would give any Fae hunter more power to use if they were to make an attempt."

"Where is the Kitsune anyway?" I asked. "He said he'd be here."

Warren leaned out the open window and gave the air a sniff. "Not anywhere close to us. But that doesn't mean he's not around. He said he'd find a place where he could watch the school. Those fox shifters are crafty. I wouldn't expect him to be out in the open."

"I haven't decided if I trust him yet or not. I don't like the way he snuck up on Sadie's home that way."

"The background checks I've put out on him have all come back clean, Rose. His backstory checks out and I haven't been able to poke any holes in anything he's said. If he's lying, he's one of the best I've ever met."

"He's a Kitsune. It goes with the territory."

Warren chuckled to himself.

"What's so funny?"

"I'm thinking of all the things that go with the territory with you."

My jaw dropped for a second. "Like what?"

"Paranoia for one. You know not everyone or everything is trying to kill you, Rose."

"It's not me I'm worried about. Pay attention to the people coming and going from the school tonight. I'm sure something is going to happen here. The school is the center of this whole thing. I first spotted him trailing a bus and we know Sadie and Chip will be here tonight."

Warren muttered something under his breath.

"What?" I asked.

"I still think you should have told Chip about what you thought about tonight. Wouldn't he be better prepared for what might happen if he knew?"

"He can't hide his feelings or keep a secret. He'd be all nervous and spook the hunter into postponing their attack. This is our chance to nab them."

"If you say so. The meeting is almost over and nothing has

happened. Maybe Godo was wrong about the timing of the next attack."

"We'll find out." I opened the driver's door. "I'm getting out. You stay here and watch the parking lot. I'm going to see if I can pick up any trail closer to the building."

I walked across the lot towards the front of the building. People started to file out as I approached. The meeting must have just ended. I moved off to the side and watched everyone as they came out. I didn't see Chip and Sadie anywhere among them. People chatted on the way to their cars and soon the lot was almost empty. There was still no sign of Chip or my niece.

I walked over to the front glass doors to peer inside. That was when I spotted them. Chip and Sadie walked towards me with a tall blonde woman who had a little blond girl skipping along beside her. Sadie chatted with the little girl, her hands moving as she described something to her friend.

My attention zeroed in on the woman who was the mother, and my eyes went wide.

Before I could move away from the doors, Chip and the woman pushed them open and walked through, holding them for the kids before letting them go.

The woman stopped as soon as she looked my way. "Rose, is that you? I haven't seen you in, well, it has to be at least fifteen years."

The voice came back to me from my past and I realized the face I stared back at was none other than my old school nemesis. We'd had a contentious relationship all through middle and high school, being from two of the prominent local Fae families.

"Patty Peyton, it has been a while, hasn't it?"

"It's actually Patricia Heraty now." She held up her left hand and flashed a large diamond ring next to her wedding band. "I see you never managed to find a man willing to put up with you. That's sad, but not entirely unpredictable."

I countered without missing a beat. "Getting married off to someone to save my family's failing fortune just so I could push out babies was never my life plan, but hey, you do you."

Patty frowned and opened her mouth to respond. Warren's shouted warning cut her off just in time for me to dive into her in my attempt to get to Sadie.

I tackled both Sadie and Patty to the pavement right before a crossbow bolt hummed through the air to shatter against the school entrance's brick wall. Chip still stood there, twisting his head back and forth searching for the source of the shot.

"Chip, you idiot. Get down here. You're a giant target."

Chip shouted and pointed across the parking lot. "There, I see someone over there." He raised up his hand, palm outward, and I felt the familiar tingle of magical energy flowing. A split second later another crossbow bolt slammed into Chip's guardian barrier. The shaft didn't shatter this time. It stuck there in midair, inches from his face.

"Can you still see him?" I asked. "Tell Warren where he is."

"I lost sight of him when I had to block the incoming shot. He was over at the edge of the parking lot, near that stand of trees." He pointed in that direction with his free hand. He kept the other one up, maintaining the barrier.

"Come over here so you can cover Sadie and Patty. I'll go and help Warren track him down. He can't have gone far from where you saw him last."

Chip crouched down beside Patty, who'd scooped her own daughter into her lap, her arms wrapped protectively around her child. Chip kept his hand out to hold the force field while he hugged Sadie close with his other arm.

Seeing they were safe, I said, "Stay here and keep the building at your back. I'll come for you once it's safe. Patty, stay here with them. You'll be safe with Chip."

Patty said something to me, but I didn't hear it. I had already taken off at a dead run for the trees at the far side of the parking lot. I didn't have time to fetch my sword, but I had pulled a silver alloy dagger from my knee-high boots. It would stand me well in a fight.

I reached the trees, calling upon my night sight to brighten the moonlight into something closer to the gloom at early dusk. I stopped and crouched to search the ground around me. I didn't see any discernible tracks though I could tell someone had knelt here to take their shots across the lot at us. The slight rise in the ground here gave a perfect vantage point.

"Warren, where are you?" I stood and looked around for my companion. I knew the attacker had fled. They wouldn't stick around after two failed shots. Still, Warren's werewolf senses might have a track on where they went.

"I'm over here. I found Godo."

That didn't sound good. I ran through the trees to find Warren standing over a crumpled form on the ground. "Oh no."

"Yes, he has a crossbow bolt in his throat. It's silver. He never had a chance. I think I heard that first shot at Godo and it warned me the hunter was over here somewhere. He repositioned after killing him and I had just spotted him on that rise when I saw you by the doors."

"He shot as soon as Sadie came out of the building. It's clear she was the target." I spun around on Warren. "If you saw him, why didn't you stop him? He got off two shots before he ran."

"Three," Warren said.

The groan of pain and the look in his eyes finally penetrated my anger at losing the chance to catch the hunter. I looked closer at Warren and saw the thumb-thick feathered end of a crossbow bolt sticking out from between his ribs. He clutched at the wound with both hands, trying to stop the bleeding.

"Damnit, Warren. Why didn't you say something?"

"You never—" he paused to gasp, "gave me the chance."

I sheathed my dagger and ducked my head under his arm to help him stand. "Come on. We've got to get you to the hospital."

"No, pull it out. I'll heal up after, but I can't with the silver inside me."

"Are you sure?" I wasn't squeamish, but there were perfectly good doctors at the county hospital. Some were friendly to Unusuals and would keep Warren's secret.

"Do it. Hurry. I'm losing too much blood."

I reached out and wrapped my fingers around the feathered shaft. "Let's do this on three, okay? One. Two. Three!" I twisted and pulled straight back with all my strength. The shaft pulled free easily. The head was a conical penetrating cone and not the traditional barbed hunting head. If Warren had been hit in a vital spot, he'd have been dead before he hit the ground. He was lucky.

Warren pressed his hand across the hole as soon as the bolt pulled free. He pushed hard to staunch the flow of blood, though some leaked through his fingers.

"You sure you don't want to go in and get stitched up? Even with your werewolf regeneration, you're going to need a few days to bounce back from that."

He shook his head. "I'll be fine. I'll go back to the car. You go and check on Sadie and Chip. The kids shouldn't see me with all this blood everywhere."

Warren left me standing there, and I tried to decide what to do about Godo's body. I opted to leave it where it was. I'd call it in to a friend on the local Sheriff's force. They could send someone out after a dead body was found near the elementary school. I'd do that after I got Sadie out of here. I didn't want her around the school any more tonight. We didn't need the attention drawn to the family by indicating there'd even been an attack on us.

I groaned inside a little as I remembered who else was back with Sadie and Chip. That meant I had to go back and deal with Patty Peyton, or Heraty, or whatever her name was. I needed an excuse that would keep her quiet about it, too. She didn't know who our family really was, just that we were also descended from Fae nobles who'd traveled to the new world a few centuries before. I needed to keep it that way.

By the time I got closer to the school, I heard Patty fawning over Chip. Some things never changed, even after she was married. They sat on the ground by the entrance. Chip still maintained his barrier and looked to be close to drained of mana for holding it this long.

"Chip," Patty said. "When I found out you were Sadie's uncle, I assumed you were just a plain old human. I didn't realize you had powers of your own. What are you, some kind of warlock?"

"Uh, yeah, something like that. I was asked to take over as the kids' guardian after their parents died."

"I'll bet that really pissed off Rose," Patty replied.

I strode into the pool of light by the school's front entrance. "I've gotten over it. Chip and I share the duties now." I pointed at Chip's minivan parked nearby. "It's safe to let the barrier down. You should get out of here. Go straight home and get Sadie to bed. Send Ms. McGarry home and thank her for watching Addy tonight. I'll call you to make sure you're safe."

"What are you going to do?" Chip asked.

"I'm going to stay here and make sure Patty and her daughter are okay and know how to keep a secret."

"We're fine, and it's Patricia." Patty bristled as she took her daughter's hand and stood up.

I didn't respond to her until Chip and Sadie loaded up the minivan and left to go home. "Patty, you don't know what you're dealing with here. There's someone dangerous in town hunting Fae nobles and I'm worried they're after Sadie."

"Sadie?" Patty laughed. "Why would anyone come after your has-been family? It's obvious they were after me or my Astrid. We're the local Fae nobility of note."

I rolled my eyes. "Good gods, Patty, how do you still have your enormous ego? Most people mature out of that kind of thing."

"You're just jealous that I have all the things you were never able to have. Your sister had them and even she wasn't good enough to hold on to happiness. What makes you think you can have it by taking away mine?"

"You take that back about Lili." My hands balled up into fists at my side. "Take it back now."

Patty glanced down at my clenched hands and smiled. "No need to go medieval about it, Rose. That was always your problem. You were such a hot head back in school. It seems you haven't grown out of your high school faults either." She walked past me. "Look, I thank you for saving us back there. I'll alert our family about the hunter. We have our own resources to protect us. We don't need you to do it for us."

I stood there with my jaw dropped as she walked out to her car. She loaded Astrid into the back seat and drove her sedan from the school's parking lot. I watched her go and then remembered Warren sitting injured in my car. I rushed back to the Firebird. Right before I left the lot, I called in the report of Godo's body to my friend in the Sheriff's office. He agreed to come and take care of it. With everything wrapped up here, I drove Warren home. I'd stay with him long enough to patch up his wound and make sure he was settled with enough food to fuel his regeneration, then I'd get back out and look for our hunter.

# 9

# Chip

Rose and I had training the next day at the dojo. It was during school hours, right after the bus picked up Sadie. I brought Addy along and planned to settle him down with a tablet playing videos he liked. That would buy me some time to spar with Rose.

She waited out in front for me. A single glance down at her watch when I walked up told me she considered me late to the training. That wouldn't bode well for how she'd handle things for the next hour. Still, I didn't have to take it without a fight.

Inside, I grabbed one of the wooden practice blades on the way by the entrance and settled Addy down with my tablet. He sat cross-legged on the floor and held it in his lap, grinning from ear to ear. He loved our training days for this reason alone. He got all the screen time he wanted while we practiced with our weapons.

"How did things go with Patricia after I left?" I asked while I worked through some forms to stretch with the wooden blade.

"As usual, Patty thinks everything is all about her. She's sure the hunter was after her and her daughter."

I thought about it and asked, "Could they be?"

"No, of course not. Sadie is the future Fae queen. She's the one they're after. You know they trailed the bus after our stop. That's the only explanation." She stopped her stretching and pointed at the center of the mat. "Let's begin. I have a lot to work out and you're going to help me."

I winced at the thought of sparring with angry Rose but knew there was no way around it. Rose waited in the middle of the mat and beckoned to me. I held my sword in a low guard position as I advanced. It was a good thing I was ready. She began her attack before I'd gone two steps forward.

Spinning around, I brought the sword up and blocked her incoming thrust at my midsection but only barely. Knowing she'd have a follow-up attack, I pressed forward instead of just holding my ground. It was better to be in close where my larger, stronger frame could be used to the greatest advantage.

My advance made Rose have to back-pedal and change her planned attack to a blocking parry of her own as I swept my blade around to slash at her ribs.

Clack! The two wooden practice blades met and slid off each other. I had pressed the attack, but Rose had more than one trick up her sleeve. She switched to short, jabbing thrusts with her sword. They forced me to back up as I couldn't easily get my longer blade around each time to bat her attacks aside.

Then I made my first mistake. I kept my blade moving around to parry another of the short thrusts, except Rose changed up the pattern and hesitated just a hair's breadth. It was enough for my parry to swish through thin air right before she shoved her blunted tip forward into my ribs.

"Oooof" The grunt escaped me as her blade drove the air from my lungs right before I doubled over in pain. I dropped to my knees, clutching my midsection and gasping to catch my breath. "Damnit, Rose. You need. To work. This out. Another way." I sucked in a breath between each phrase as I sought to re-inflate my lungs.

"You're just too slow. Get up, let's try it again."

I shook my head. "No, not until you tell me what it is about Patricia that's got you all ganked up."

She glared down at me. "You wouldn't understand, Chip. You're a guy."

"Try me. I can channel my feminine side with the best of them."

"It's not about that. Patty's been my nemesis since seventh grade. She teamed up with a group of other girls and decided she didn't need to be my friend anymore. She wanted to be popular more than keep our friendship going."

"So what? Rose, that was years ago. You've grown up into a total badass. You run around with a sword killing evil creatures and demons. She's a soccer mom in suburbia. It's not even a competition. You win."

"See, I told you you wouldn't understand." She pointed with the end of her sword. "Get up. Let's do it again."

I stood, but I wasn't giving up on getting Rose to see herself the way I saw her. "Has she got some sort of dirt on you? Is that why you're angry about meeting up with her after so long?"

Rose didn't answer, instead she charged forward, leading with her blade.

I never had a chance. Before I knew what hit me, she'd swept my back leg to the side, twisting my ankle in the process. I went down hard to the mat. Her blade poked me between my shoulder blades for good measure.

I rolled over. "Rose, that's enough. I'm not here to be your personal punching bag. If you want to take some angst out, do it against the sparring post over there. I'm here to learn and the only thing I'm learning right now is to not let you spar with me for a while."

She stared down at me, breathing hard with her sword still extended in my direction. "She made my life a living hell. It was bad enough I had to follow Lili through school. She was always the golden child. Homecoming queen, prom queen, class president, she had it all. Then along came Rose, the little sister. Rose likes to wear black and listen to alternative music. She isn't a popular girl like her sister and even the teachers decided to treat me as someone less deserving because I wasn't more like Lili."

I tried to understand, but it was hard. I was the guy who dated girls like Lili in high school. I was the star quarterback and the one everyone looked up to. It was why everyone was surprised when my younger brother, Bobby, landed the prettiest girl in college and brought her home to marry. That was supposed to be me.

"Rose, tell me what Patricia did that was so bad to you? I need to understand." I stopped and met her eyes. "Really, I want to know."

She kept staring at me until the tip of her blade dipped and she turned around, wiping at her eyes with her sleeve. "It wasn't just one thing. She and her friends made it a point to make my every moment in school harder than it needed to be."

"But you had all that training, Rose. Why didn't you just kick her ass and be done with it? She'd have left you alone after that."

"That's how guys solve problems, Chip. You fight and then shake hands and everything's fine. With girls it's different. I couldn't fight her. First, I was afraid I'd go too far and really hurt her. I had the skills, after all. Second, it would have only proven to everyone I was the freak Patty said I was."

She wiped at her face again before she turned around to face me. I took the opportunity to get back to my feet.

"Rose, you're not that girl anymore. Patty isn't in a position of power over you. Even as the president of the PTA, she…"

"She's the president of the school's PTA?" Rose threw her hands in the air. "Of course she is. I should have known. This is how she'll get back at me again. She'll take it out on Sadie, I just know it."

"She won't do anything of the sort," I replied. "She even invited Sadie over to a play date at her house with Astrid. The two girls seem to have become friends at school."

"No way." Rose's eyes flashed that bright emerald green that said she'd filled herself with power. "I forbid it, Chip."

I needed to stand my ground on this one. "Well, then, it's a good thing you're not Sadie's Guardian. I am. It's good for her to make friends, especially among other Unusuals and Fae kids. She needs to know how to act in this human world. They can learn together and support each other."

"Chip, Patty only did this to get back at me. She has something up her sleeve. I wouldn't trust that Astrid either."

"Listen to yourself, Rose. You just accused a six-year-old girl of being untrustworthy because her mother was a mean girl in high school. Astrid is a little Fae girl. She's just like Sadie. They have a lot in common and I think it'll be good for both of them to play together once in a while."

Rose lowered her voice to a whisper and turned away. "Do what you want, Chip. You're right, I can't stop you. I think this training session is over." She walked over to the rack and placed her sword in its home. "You should take Addy home and plan your little date with Patty and her daughter."

She crossed to the door and walked out. I watched her get in her Firebird and back out of her parking spot before driving away. I leaned on the sword like a cane while I limped on my sprained ankle over to the dojo's office door.

"Hey, Mike, we're done for the day. Thanks for coming in and opening up early for us."

"No problem. I had paperwork to do before my first self-defense class anyway."

A thought occurred to me. "You've lived here a long time. Did you happen to go to school with Rose and Patty Peyton?"

Mike nodded. "I was a year behind them. I hung out more with the crowd Rose ran in than the popular kids. It was bad, Chip. Rose has every reason to be mad at the way Patty treated her all those years ago. Patty never missed an opportunity to make fun of Rose back in school."

"Good to know," I replied. "Thanks for the information. Expect us back the regular time this Friday morning."

Mike, I discovered, was a minotaur in human form, who had also been a special forces soldier. He smiled and waved as he returned to his computer to finish up his work.

I limped over and put my practice blade back, then scooped up Addy and the tablet to head back home. I'd have to think about this whole Rose and Patty problem. It wasn't like I could just not be around her. I'd been appointed to head up the PTA carnival committee for this fall's biggest fund-raising event. As president, she could appoint whoever she wanted. She'd chosen me primarily because of my deep pockets and connections in the broader business community to help make the event a success.

I'd left the part about the carnival chairmanship out of my conversation with Rose because I knew she'd find a way to twist Patty's reasons for choosing me. I didn't want to have another fight about something completely different every time we talked about school and the PTA meetings I'd committed to attending. Part of me hoped Rose would put it behind her, but then I reminded myself that she never forgot anything.

---

## 10

## Rose

---

I never thought I'd revisit the feelings that followed me through most of high school. It had been a dark time for me. The teachers heard Lili Eldersdottir's little sister was coming up through the grades and they all expected another star student and leader. What they got was me, the strange, goth girl who liked thick black eyeliner, piercings, and alternative music. I wasn't a good fit for the standard suburban public school system. Add in students like Patty Peyton, who picked out anything and anyone who was different, and it was a recipe for nightmares when you were the odd kid out.

A primal shout came out from the depths of my soul and my foot pressed down on the accelerator. I wove in and out of traffic, screaming at the injustice of a world that would bring her back into my life again. I stopped when I came to a red traffic light. I looked to one side and realized the young woman driving next to me had noticed me yelling as I pulled to a stop.

The light turned green, and I punched the accelerator again, peeling out from the intersection to get away from the woman's judgmental expression. At least I wasn't screaming at the top of my lungs anymore.

My phone rang and I picked up. It was Warren.

"Rose, I found some things in Godo's car I thought you should see. Do you have some time this morning?"

"As it turns out, I just had part of my calendar clear out. Tell me where you are."

He wasn't that far away from me. I pulled into the left turn lane and hung a U-turn to come back around and head in his direction. He was at the community pond, which gave us a good place to chat where people wouldn't easily overhear us.

I parked the Firebird and walked over to where Warren sat on a park bench by the pond. He was throwing bits of bread into the water, feeding the ducks.

"Isn't a werewolf feeding ducks kind of like putting out bait for your dinner?"

"I don't like wild duck. Too gamey."

I looked around. I didn't see his car. I sat down beside him. "How'd you get here?"

"I drove Godo's car. He doesn't need it anymore and I didn't want the police to take all the evidence inside. There's information exposing half the Fae nobility in the U.S., including yours."

The hairs rose on the back of my neck. "He knew about Sadie's identity?"

"I don't think so. He only listed your branch as a 'significant segment' from the old country. I think he was trying to get ahead of the hunter, which was how he found Lili's neighborhood, at least that's my theory."

I didn't like mysteries. They bothered me at an elemental level. When those mysteries involved my family, I became super protective. "Good job taking the car. Do you think the police are looking for it?"

"Possibly. Godo was living in it. He'd checked out of his motel room so there was nothing there for the police to find. Let them figure it out on their own. I'll clean out the information about Unusuals, wipe it down, and leave it somewhere they'll find it. That should close the case from their standpoint. I think they're going to write it off as a hunting accident."

My eyebrows shot up. "In the middle of town next to an elementary school? A hunting accident there?"

"That's what my buddy said. They can't find any evidence of anything else around the school. No one but you, Chip, and Patty witnessed the crossbow attack so there's nothing to tie the incident to anything else. I thought you'd be happy."

"I am, I'm just distracted, that's all. This whole Patty situation is getting under my skin."

"Yeah, I remember how she and her friends treated you in school. They were real assholes back then. But people change, you know. She's grown up, married, and has kids now. Maybe you should give her a chance."

"I don't think I will," I replied. "She's set her sights on Chip it appears. She's roped him into joining the PTA at the school. He didn't just attend the meeting. I'll bet he's on some committee now."

"Ooo, how diabolical. What evil will she perpetrate next? Maybe she'll raise money for a new playground. That would be awful."

"Oh, shut up, Warren. I didn't come here to listen to you make fun of me."

He did as he was told and returned to sitting quietly feeding the ducks. After a minute, I held out my hand and he tore off a hunk of the loaf for me to get in on the fun. I found it strangely calming. The ducks seemed to float serenely across the water, but when they came near the shore, I could see their little webbed feet paddling fiercely beneath the water to propel them after the floating bits of bread.

I pulled some more bread chunks free and tossed them one at a time into the pond. The ducks competed for the food, and I found myself trying to place the tossed pieces in the middle of groups to see who would come up with the food each time.

"You said you found the background on the Fae families," I asked after a few minutes of silence. "Did you discover anything that might point to who the hunter is? He must have had some clues if he tracked him this far."

"There was a flyer from a club in Baltimore. I had to look it up online. I'm not the type to go clubbing in the city anymore."

"And? What did you find?"

"It's a place that caters to Unusuals and the human groupies they attract."

I rolled my eyes. "So, vamp bunnies."

"And others like them," he said. He pulled out the flyer from a pocket and handed it to me. "Mostly, it seems above board, but it might be worth checking out. It's a relatively new club. It just popped up in the last few years. I think if I check around, I can wrangle us an invitation. That's the only way in."

"Then you and I will have to pay this place a visit." I studied the unfolded flyer. Proto Sapiens offered a ladies night this coming Friday. There was no cover for women and their guest. "This weekend's event looks like a perfect opportunity."

"Not me, Rose. One of the primary rules of the place is everyone has to bring their own human sub to the club. I guess making sure everyone has their own subservient human tagging along is a way to keep the riff-raff out."

I read the fine print about guests at the bottom of the flyer and snorted a laugh. "That's also a good way to keep the authorities from finding out you're doing bad things. It would be hard to sneak in an undercover cop if they had to show up accompanied by someone else all the time. Very smart when you think about it."

Warren let a half grin cross his face.

"What?" I asked.

"You know what this means, Rose?"

"No, what?"

"If you want to investigate this place, you're going to have to bring Chip along."

"Oh, he'll love that. I'm sure he was into some kinky sex clubs up in New York. This'll be right up his alley." I didn't relish bringing him along, but if it helped me find out what Godo discovered there, I might be able to flush out the hunter before he had a chance to strike again. I wondered how he'd gotten inside if he didn't know any humans around. I promptly decided I didn't need to know. Godo was dead and anything he did that might have crossed a line didn't matter anymore.

I finished feeding the ducks what I had from the chunk of bread Warren had given me, then I got up. "I should probably check in and make sure Chip's okay. I was pretty rough with him at the dojo this morning."

Warren chuckled.

"Oh, shut up. It wasn't like that at all."

"I didn't say a word. What happens between the two of you is all right by me."

"Nothing happens between us. I'm just training him, and I took out my frustrations on him. That's all."

"Cause any permanent damage?" Warren asked.

"I don't think so. He limped a little at the end, but I'm sure he'll bounce back from that. His Guardian abilities speed up his healing. It's not regeneration like you have, but he should be okay in a few days."

"Perfect. He'll be better just in time for the weekend and your little outing to the club. Maybe he can get a little leather biker outfit between now and then."

I caught Warren's smirk, and I punched him lightly in the shoulder. "That's enough of that. We will need some sort of costume, though, for a place like this. I'll have to think on it."

"Are you going to consult with Chip?"

"No, he wouldn't know what was expected in a place like this."

Warren laughed. "And you would?"

"I'll have you know I have been to quite a few clubs of dubious nature in my day. I've traveled the world hunting evil artifacts, remember. You don't do that and not learn how to blend in among certain crowds."

Warren held up his hands palm out in surrender. "I'm sure you'll do fine. I'm going to go finish cleaning out Godo's car, then I'll drop a dime to the Sheriff's Department and let them know where it is."

"Good," I said. "I'll go and apologize to Chip. Keep in touch if anything else from Godo's car pans out."

Warren nodded and we left for our cars. When I got inside the Firebird, I called Chip on the phone. He picked up on the fourth ring.

"Hey, Rose. Did you decide I needed a verbal beating, too?"

I winced. "No, actually, I called to tell you I was sorry for being a little rough this morning."

He gasped on the other end of the phone. "Hold everything. Are you really apologizing to me? I need to pull over so I can write down the date and time. This must be some sort of holiday."

"Very funny, Chip. I'm being serious. How's your ankle?"

"I took something for the pain and swelling. It's not as bad as it might have been."

"That's good." I decided to pitch the club idea to him. "Maybe I could make it up to you by taking you to a club in Baltimore this weekend. I got a lead from Warren I need to follow up there, and you and I could go and have a good time while we're at it."

"It's been a long time since I've been clubbing. I had to leave that whole life behind. You know that."

"Are you saying no?" I asked.

"No, but we'll need a sitter and it's late to find one for this weekend. Sammi is still away helping her sick mother."

"I'll see if Ms. McGarry is available. She had a good time with the kids the last time."

"We need to get another regular sitter, Rose. We can't keep using your aunt's cook."

I ignored him and said, "I'll pick you up at seven on Friday. It's a themed club so I'll send you something to wear."

"What kind of club is it? I'm getting the sense there's something you're not telling me."

I realized I needed to come clean, so I filled him in on everything Warren had told me and I told him about the flyer. "We need to go in as a team and I need you on board to act like I brought you and not the other way around. Are you okay with that?"

"Sure, it might be fun to let you take the lead and buy me drinks and dinner for a change. I'm in. As long as whatever I'm wearing won't freak out the kids, I'll do it."

"Good. Then I'll see you Friday. Maybe we'll track down the hunter once and for all."

I hung up and felt a little better about myself for the first time since my run-in with Patty. Chip and I had fallen into a good place of give and take where it came to guarding the kids. I didn't want to do anything to mess that up. Friday would be a chance to make sure we were really good. I smiled and drove back to my apartment to get a shower and face the rest of the day.

# 11

# Chip

My ankle felt better in a few days, and I wasn't limping at all when the time came for me and the kids to go over to Patty's house one afternoon to visit. The official reason for the visit was to have a play date for Astrid and Sadie. School was off for a teacher training day so the kids could hang out at home together. The alternative reason to get together was to spend some time going over some new ideas for the PTA carnival in a month. If there was an alternative to the alternative, it had to do with some pretty obvious vibes I picked up when I talked on the phone with her the previous evening. I smiled and decided to see where that took us. It would be nice to try and date again without worrying about hiding all the magical world from them.

I filed away my thoughts about anything romantic and tried to focus on the upcoming fundraising event. The former carnival chairperson had moved away after they'd set up most of the event in advance. Many of the details were planned during the previous carnival with the company that brought the rides and attractions. All I needed to do was to coordinate the volunteers and add a few finishing touches. I was looking forward to adding my special Chip Proctor panache to what had been a pretty ordinary event in the past. Patty thought those extra flourishes might lend to the event's even bigger success.

I brought my laptop along with Addy's diaper bag. He still wore pull-ups most of the time. He wasn't getting the idea around potty training yet. Patty had a son a little older than Addy was, so we'd let them sit next to each other on the floor. Kids that age didn't really play together but they'd be able to keep busy enough for Patty and me to get our work done.

My phone buzzed and I picked up when I saw it was her calling. "I hope this isn't a cancelation call. I was looking forward to coming over to your place today."

"My husband is working from home today and needs the house quiet this afternoon. I thought we could meet at the park near the development. The kids can play, and we can work on one of the picnic tables."

My expectations sank a little when I heard about her husband. I'd heard they were estranged, but apparently, he still lived at home. Pushing aside my disappointment at finding out he was still at least partially in the picture, I said, "The park would be a great idea. I'll bring along a cooler with some drinks for us and the kids."

"Good," Patty said. "I'll bring some snacks to fill out the play date."

"Same time, two o'clock?" I asked.

"Yep, see you there. Me and the kids are looking forward to it."

I smiled and hung up.

Sadie had heard me on the phone and came out from where she'd been sitting and reading in the family room. "Are we still going over to Astrid's house, Uncle Chip?"

"Change of plans. We're still getting together with them, but at the park instead. We'll pack up the big wagon with some toys and maybe a soccer ball, then we can walk over after lunch."

Sadie's worried expression shifted to a big grin. "Good, I was worried I wouldn't get to see Astrid."

"What do you like most about Astrid?"

"Mostly, I like that we're both Fae. We have to hide that side of ourselves in school. It's nice to talk about how we're both princesses."

My eyes widened. Sadie wasn't supposed to talk about her royal connections. "But you're the real princess. You can't let anyone know that, right?"

"I know, but Astrid says she is through her family, too."

That caught me by surprise. I didn't know enough about Fae genealogy and succession to understand all the titles for the nobles and stuff. Rose was pretty adamant that Sadie was the only future Fae queen. If there were others who had a claim, that could make things difficult later on. I would have to ask Rose about that the next time I saw her. Maybe I could probe Patty's relationship to royalty, too, without letting on too much about who Sadie was.

"Sadie, what have you told Astrid about you being a princess? This is important."

"I told her you call me princess, that's all. You said I couldn't tell them about Mommy and Aunt Rose being royalty. It would be weird to talk about that anyway. No one goes around calling themselves royalty. This is America."

"That's right. Just remember to keep it all a secret. I'll talk to Aunt Rose about Astrid being a princess. Maybe it's just because she's called that at home, too."

"No, she said her mother told her she was a real princess from way back in her family. She's telling the truth. I came home and looked it up in Aunt Allura's book. All the Fae noble houses are in there."

"Really?" I asked. "Can you show me where you found it?"

Sadie nodded and led me over to the tall bookshelf against the wall. I pulled down the large, leather-bound book and set it on the dining room table. Sadie climbed on a chair and flipped it open, going through the pages until she stopped on one in particular.

"See?" She stabbed a finger down to point out an entry. "There's Astrid's family. It says they're royalty, too."

I leaned forward to read the ornate text in the magical tome. There was Astrid at the bottom of the page. There was a glowing crown over her entry.

I looked back up the page to see Patricia Peyton Heraty with a "princess" designation beside her name. The little crown symbol floated next to all the women of the line all the way up the page to the beginning. I flipped a few pages back until I found the page with Lili and Rose's family on it. There were no floating crowns beside their names or princess designations. An asterisked note at the bottom of the page stated the family was a Lesser Noble House. I hadn't noticed that the last time I looked at it.

I wondered why there were no references to Sadie being the next queen or Rose and Lili being princesses. I'd heard people like the family counselor address them that way. It made no sense. I needed to ask Rose for some clarification. Something strange was going on here and I didn't pretend to understand all the lore involved. I marked the page with a junk mail flyer from the pile on the end of the dining room table and closed the book.

"Let's go and make lunch so we'll be ready to go play when the time comes to meet up with Astrid."

She followed me into the kitchen and helped me make peanut butter sandwiches for the two kids. I mixed up a salad of some fresh lettuce and veggies I had in the fridge for myself. Fifteen minutes later, I'd set us up at the table in the kitchen to eat lunch. Sadie and Addy finished in record time, and both asked when it was time to go play.

I decided we could head over to the playground early. I packed up the wagon with a cooler of water bottles and an ice pack. Then I grabbed Sadie's soccer ball from the back yard to toss in for good measure. We left the house and headed down the street to the big neighborhood playground at the edge of our development. Addy rode in the wagon. He kept calling out "Mush, Unca Chip. Mush." We all laughed when I barked like a dog.

The playground was a few blocks away. It had the usual equipment for kids of various ages as well as several multipurpose playing fields the rec council leagues used at different times of the year for a variety of sports from lacrosse, to soccer, to field hockey. It was nice to have it close enough to get out and walk to when we needed a break from our own yard.

Sadie bounced along at my side. She barely hid her excitement at being able to hang out with Astrid for a few hours. I pulled the wagon while wearing my backpack holding my laptop. I hoped the kids let Patty and I get some work finished.

To my surprise, she was already there. She'd arrived early, too. I waved and she waved back. She'd set up at a picnic table beside the smallest of the three playground areas. This one was sized well for people Addy's size. This way we could keep an eye on Addy and Astrid's little brother, Clayton.

I pulled the wagon up beside the table and lifted the plastic cooler up onto the table. "Hey, Patty— I mean Patricia, I see you opted to come over early, too."

She laughed. "You can call me Patty if you want. Rose does it so why shouldn't you." She nodded at Sadie and Addy. "Let me guess. The kids raced through their lunch so they could meet up here and play?"

"On the nose," I said, tapping my right nostril. I laughed along with her. The two girls grabbed the soccer ball and moved over to an open space to kick it back and forth.

Addy climbed down from the wagon and pointed to nearby equipment where Patty's son played already. "Unca Chip, play?"

"Sure, Addy, I'll walk over and play with you." Patty joined me and we followed Addy to the steps up to a low platform. There was a straight slide down and a bridge over to another platform with a curvy slide.

Addy climbed up the steps. Clayton slid down the straight slide and Addy moved to the top to do the same.

"Sit down, first, buddy. Remember?"

He smiled at me and plopped down on his butt before sliding down to the rubber mulch at the bottom. He laughed and ran around to do it again. I knew from experience; this would keep him occupied for a while.

Patty came over and stood by my side. A whiff of her floral perfume wafted my way.

"Do you want to talk some about the carnival?" I asked. I was still unsure about the husband situation.

"Sure, the boys will be okay here together and we'll be close by. Did you bring your computer? I can set up a hotspot for you if you need to connect."

"I've got one, too. Addy will be fine with Clayton. We'll sit on the other side of the table so we can keep an eye on them."

We moved back to the table about fifteen feet away and sat facing the playground. After I pulled out my laptop, I connected to my phone and started by opening a spreadsheet she had sent me. She plopped down next to me and leaned close to see my screen. It was all quite nice.

We talked about the event and possible attractions available for about fifteen minutes. Sadie and Astrid came over to the table with their soccer ball. Both had their hair plastered around their faces from exertion. They'd been playing hard, trying to out-dribble each other.

"Can we have some water?"

"Sure," I said. "There are water bottles in the cooler. Just one each. There's enough for everyone."

Sadie lifted the lid on the small cooler and screamed as water sprayed all over her in an explosion from inside the container.

It took me a second to realize what had caused it. Then I spotted the quivering, feathered end of a crossbow bolt protruding from the side of the cooler. The thick foam and plastic had saved Sadie's life.

"Everybody get on the ground. NOW!" My shout came out almost as a scream of fear. I scanned the area while I opened myself up to my Guardian magic. Where had it come from?

I spotted the dark sedan with the tinted windows from the first day of school parked in the gravel lot over by the playing fields. I raised the shield in that direction and spread it as wide as I could. I didn't see the hunter, but he must be around somewhere.

Movement to the right drew my searching eyes. I saw a figure in black pants and a bulky, black coat crouched by the end of aluminum bleachers near the playing fields. They held something in their arms. I realized it was a reloaded crossbow just in time to twist around and place my barrier between us and the incoming bolt.

The speeding missile ricocheted off my shield and stuck in the grass between us and the hunter. The black-clad figure stood. He was shorter than I'd expected. He stood and stared at us for a few seconds and then ran for his car.

Without a second thought, I focused my will on the power of my shield, shrinking down the focus of it to a pinpoint. I tracked after the fleeing hunter with my eyes. After they took two more running strides towards the sedan, I let the focused rod of power go.

"Yes!" I pumped my fist at my side.

The attacker stumbled, clutched at their leg, and toppled to the ground.

"Patty, get the kids to safety." I didn't wait to see if she heard me. I raced across the playing field between me and the collapsed hunter. I was halfway across the field when he got back to his feet and hobbled to the parked car. I kept running after him.

Seconds later the car peeled out in a spray of gravel that left me holding my arms in front of my face to shield myself from the incoming shower of stones.

When I put my arms down, the car had sped away onto the main street running by the development. I looked around to see if there were any clues to the identity of the mystery attacker. The crossbow lay on the grass nearby. A bolt lay on the ground beside the cocked and ready weapon. He was ready for another shot when I hit him with my bolt of power. We were lucky.

I picked up the bow and the bolt. Maybe Rose or Warren could use it to track down the hunter. It was worth a shot at least.

On the way back to the picnic table where Patty crouched with the four kids, I realized my arms were bleeding from the sharp gravel kicked up by the car's spinning wheels. Patty spotted the injury about the same time I did.

"Chip, you're hurt." She stood and grabbed some napkins from her snack bag. She ran over to me and started blotting at the bloody cuts dotting my forearms. Before I knew what was happening, she'd stopped tending to my injuries and pulled me into a tight embrace then locked her lips on mine.

After a few long and not unpleasant seconds, she let go and stepped away. She used the napkins balled up in her hands to blot at tears streaming down her face.

"What's wrong, Patty? Are you okay? If you're worried about the kiss, I won't tell your husband."

"I don't care about him. He's getting ready to move out anyway. I was thinking that's the second time you've used your power to save my life, Chip. Clearly, they were attacking me or Astrid. Besides, I didn't mind the kiss. Did you?"

A flush flashed across my face. I hated when I blushed. I turned away and searched for Sadie. Patty thought she was the object of the attack, but I knew otherwise. Sadie had been right there when the bolt slammed into the cooler beside her.

My niece held onto Addy on the other side of the picnic table, her eyes wide as she stared at me. "Are you all right, Uncle Chip? You're bleeding."

"I'm fine. Nothing a little ointment and some bandages won't take care of. How about you and Addy. Are you two good?"

She nodded, her dark ponytail bobbing behind her.

I turned back to Patty who was still dabbing at her eyes. "I'm glad you're okay, Patty. I need to get the kids home and safe, then I need to call Rose. She'll know what to do. You should probably do the same thing."

"What? Call Rose?" Patty smiled. "She's not my Fae warrior wannabe. She's yours."

"No, I meant do you need me to call someone to pick you up or do you feel up to walking?"

"I drove. My SUV is over there." She pointed at the lot opposite the lot where the attacker had parked. "Can I give you three a lift home? That's a long walk if that maniac is still out there."

Seeing she had a big enough car, I nodded. "That would be great. I don't feel comfortable out in the open on the sidewalk right now."

We climbed in the large SUV. It had three rows of seats so there was plenty of room inside for all of us. I fretted over not having car seats or boosters for the kids, but we weren't going far. Soon, we pulled up in front of our house.

Patty laid a hand on mine where it sat on the center console arm rest. Her thumb stroked the inside of my palm. "Thank you, Chip. I won't forget this." Her eyes had a smoky look to them and if I didn't know better, I'd swear they'd started to glow a deep azure blue.

Breaking whatever Fae magic she'd called up, I gently pulled my hand free. "It was nothing. I would've done it for anyone. We couldn't let that person keep shooting at us, right?"

I opened my door and climbed down to the street. It took a bit of time to get my kids, and all our stuff, out from the back. Patty waved, blew a kiss my way, and drove off. I looked around for signs the hunter might be close by and then ushered the kids inside as fast as I could. I wanted to get Sadie and Addy behind the house's magical wards as soon as possible. Then I had to call Rose. She'd want to know about the new attack. She'd know what to do next.

# 12

# Rose

After Chip called me about the attack, Warren and I spent the next two days searching for the hunter in all the unlikely places. We'd already exhausted the likely ones. Chip insisted he'd somehow injured the hunter's leg, though he wasn't clear on how he'd done it. I used that information and reached out to local ERs and urgent care centers for a man coming in with a leg injury in the last twenty-four hours. I had contacts in all of them from inside the Unusual community. I told them there was a rogue hunter on the loose and they were only too happy to help my search. However, none of it panned out. Once again, the culprit had disappeared as if they'd teleported away.

Finally, after forty-eight hours of no luck, Friday night arrived. I shifted gears to our outing at the club in Baltimore. This was the only thing we had that was anywhere near a warm lead. I had to believe it would turn into something more substantial.

The outfit I chose was one I hadn't worn out in a long time. I donned a pair of tight black leather pants with a matching halter top. I topped it off with a black leather biker cap, pulling the brim low over my eyes. I assessed the whole thing in the mirror and decided it needed the right accessory to make it perfect. I dug in the back of my closet until I came out with a leather riding crop. I snapped it down against my leg, savoring the slight sting.

Perfect.

Now, to go and pick up Chip. I'd given him specific instructions on what I wanted him to wear. It had to match up with the type of sub my character would be drawn to. I wanted to draw a little attention, but not enough that someone would see through our disguises. It was a stretch to think Chip could act submissive to anyone. That was the one potential error in my plan. I'd have to keep an eye on him and make sure he stayed in character. Maybe I'd even get to use the riding crop. My grin spread across my face as I left my apartment for the house.

I pulled up out front of their place in my Firebird and hopped out. The neighbor was out with electric clippers, trimming up some errant branches on the hedge between his property and Chip's. I caught him staring my way and gave him a sly wink. I could barely contain a laugh when he lost control of the trimmer for a second and hacked a big hole in the hedge. It served his wandering eyes right.

Chip waited inside for me. He was finishing up tying the plaid bow tie I'd added to the outfit I'd sent him. He smiled as I came in.

"What do you think, Rose?" He turned in a circle dressed as a nerdy professor type, right down to the yellow and brown tweed jacket with leather elbow patches. He'd even added the plain, wire-rimmed glasses to round out the whole look.

"That is perfect, Chip. If I didn't know any better, I'd think you were looking forward to this. I haven't uncovered a secret desire in you, have I?" I punctuated my questions with a snap of my riding crop against my leg.

"No, but role play is always fun as long as there's a safe word." He winked. "What's yours, Rose?"

I rolled my eyes. "There won't be a need for a safe word, Chip. Tonight is all about uncovering the identity of the hunter. That's all. Once we do that, you can go back to playing house with Patty."

"I take it you didn't have any luck finding any other clues after the attack in the park?"

"No," I replied. "But they might have gone back into the city, if that's where they're hiding out. That might be why I can't find them around here until they launch another attack. All I know is, this guy is getting on my nerves. I plan on taking them out once and for all tonight."

"Maybe we'll uncover a special clue at the club. I am a professor, after all." Chip smiled and walked over to lean around the bottom of the stairs up to the second floor. "Ms. McGarry, we're leaving. Good night, kids."

Two little voices echoed down the steps. "Good night, Uncle Chip."

"You two have fun tonight," Ms. McGarry added. She moved to the top of the stairs so she could see them both. "I've got things handled here. And I've set it up to sleep in the guest room. You two feel free to stay out as late as you want. I can leave in the morning." The little twinkle in her eye left nothing to the imagination about her thoughts about Chip and me.

Before I could reply, Chip said, "Thank you, Ms. McGarry. You're the best." He turned to me. "Shall we go?"

I waved at the cook and led the way out to my car. Soon we were on our way into the city. I took the opportunity to prep Chip for what he was about to encounter. While he was aware of the whole Unusual world, his exposure to it, especially its seedier underbelly, was very limited. The Unusuals of suburbia were much tamer than what you'd encounter in any major city, and Baltimore was no exception.

"Chip, this club is a major hang-out for vampires and others you'd know as creatures of the night. The Lord of Baltimore himself is a vamp. He has a definite twist towards the kinkier side of Unusual/human interactions. This club caters to those desires. This is why we're dressed the way we are. No one comes into this place alone. They have to bring a guest with them who is their servant of a sort, or they must pay a fee to hire one of the club's resident human subs."

"I'm familiar with the whole dominant and submissive thing, Rose," Chip countered.

I glanced over as I drove. "How familiar is that, Chip? I don't see you as the ordinary submissive type."

He frowned. "Well, I've done some reading. I never frequented the clubs of this nature in New York City, but I knew a few traders who did. I can't imagine it's all that different for the Unusual clubs that cater to the same desires."

"That's where you're wrong, Chip. There are going to be things going on that you can't freak out about."

"I'm not the type to freak out."

"So, you won't try to stop a vampire from feeding on a human in plain view of everyone in the club?"

He didn't answer right away. When he did, he asked, "Why would everyone ignore them killing a person in plain sight?"

"There won't be any killing. Most vamps are very careful, especially with their special, consensual feeder relationships. Most of them pay very well for the opportunity to feed on a live human. I know several women and men who put themselves through college, debt free, by letting a vampire keep them in a constant state of anemia for four years. All I'm saying is that it happens and it's all going to be between consenting adults."

"But how can you be sure, Rose? Don't vampires have the ability to use mind control on some people?"

"They do, but that community does a good job of policing their own for the most part. The rest of the Unusual community and the human officials who are in on our secret world make sure of that. No one wants to deal with a slew of blood-drained corpses turning up that might rise again as ravenous undead and start feeding on unsuspecting humans."

"Right, so no matter what I see, I keep my reaction to myself. I can do that. What's my role in all this tonight, then?" he asked.

"You keep your eyes open. You've seen our hunter. I haven't. Maybe something will clue you in to which one is our guy. There might be a chance to mingle with the other subs at some point. They'll probably have their own lounge to freshen up. Don't be too overt but listen to their chatter. If there's a new person in town renting subs for the night, that might be something they talk about when they think no one is paying attention."

"I'll keep my ears open. It seems like a long shot that we'd find this person on any particular night in the city. We're going to have to be pretty lucky."

"We need luck right now, Chip. We need a break, any break we can get, in this case. So far, our luck has only been enough to keep most of the hunter's targets alive. That can't hold out forever. Remember, he only has to be lucky once to kill his target."

Chip nodded. "I'll keep my eyes and ears wide open." He paused and then said, "So, it's not like I have to do anything weird with you or anything like that?"

"Gods, no!" My response might have been a little too strong, but the last thing I needed was to get entangled with Chip Proctor again. I'd relaxed my prior views about his general character over the last few years. Watching him interact with the kids the way he did had helped soften my feelings about him some, but that didn't put him in the desirable category by a long shot. Been there and done that. Never again.

Chip let out a sigh of relief that matched the one I felt inside. "That's good, Rosie. I wasn't sure what we were supposed to mean to each other in this particular situation."

"In this scenario, I'm your entire world, Chip. You do and say anything I tell you to. That is your role tonight. Don't worry. I won't make you strip for anyone, or make you lick my boots. Just keep the subservient nerdy professor vibe going. Maybe we can even have some fun with this."

"Okay, but next time, I get to be in charge."

"Seriously, Chip." I shot him a glance. "When are you not in charge?" *Or at least think you are,* I added to myself.

I let that percolate as we got onto the Jones Falls Expressway to head downtown. It wasn't far to the club at this point. The location was at the edge of the infamous Baltimore Block where all the strip clubs were located. I had no doubt Chip knew the area well from his days in the area during his college years. He was definitely the type to come to places like that with a group of friends. It would be just my luck he spotted someone he knew.

I parked the Firebird in a garage about a block away from the address and got out. Chip climbed out and I muttered a spell as I extended a hand over the roof of the sports car. The charm would keep ordinary car thieves at bay and alert me if anyone tampered with it in any way.

"Come on, Chip. Time to play our parts and find this hunter."

We walked down the street to the address. I didn't see an obvious entrance right away. It looked like a boarded-up business with vacant apartments upstairs. I was sure this was the right location. I checked my phone again for the photo I'd taken of the flyer.

Chip looked around, scanning the street on both sides. "Maybe you got the wrong address?" He walked to check out the buildings to either side.

"No, this place is the right spot. I did my homework." I stared at the building with my eyes refocused on the UV spectrum with my magically enhanced Fae vision. That changed everything. I saw the painted sign pointing to the gate between this place and the building to the left.

"Found it, Chip." I gripped the narrow chain-link gate and pulled it towards me. Three strands of barbed wire topped the six-foot tall gate to discourage people from climbing over. The gate opened easily, despite the rust all over it. I waved Chip over.

"Time to earn your keep, Chip. Remember, stay behind me and to the right at all times. I'll do all the talking. Only respond to me and no one else. We'll get through this in one piece if you follow the instructions."

He smiled and nodded down at my side. "I'll let you know if something 'crops' up."

I groaned and snapped the crop down against my leg with an audible whack. "Come on, slave."

Chip nodded and followed me into the narrow passageway between the buildings. It grew very dark, but I knew Chip could adjust his eyes the same way mine could with his Guardian magic. Hopefully, he remembered to do so before he tripped over the random pieces of trash littering the gap.

Halfway down the passage, a doorway opened in the building to the right. Three steps led down into a narrow landing with a plain steel door. There was a slot in the door at eye level and I stood in front of it with Chip behind me as I rapped on the door with the butt of my riding crop.

The slot slid open a few seconds later. A pair of glowing red eyes stared out at me, then shifted to look at Chip. I flashed a bit of my magical power to light up my emerald eyes. The person behind the door slid the slot closed as soon as I did. A second later, the door buzzed and popped open.

The thump of pounding dance music resonated deep in my chest when the door opened. A hulking figure shrouded in the shadows behind the door waved me inside. I couldn't be sure, but I thought it might be a night troll. They were a larger relative of the children's bed trolls like Bernard and Brunna. In this case, a night troll dabbled in the deep fears and nightmares of the adult human's mind. They also could be used as very effective guardians due to their ability to anticipate an attack in the split-second before it was launched.

I nodded at the figure in the shadows and said, "Come along, Chip. Don't keep me waiting." I didn't wait to see if Chip was behind me. He'd keep up. I wanted to get inside and get a sense of the scope of the place before we started looking for clues to our hunter among the patrons and guests.

The club itself was down a flight of stairs to a sub-basement that extended farther than the dimensions of the single building above. It went beneath the buildings on either side of the one through which we'd entered. Opposite the entrance, one whole side of the establishment was dedicated to private rooms. The doors lined a hallway that could only be accessed beyond a velvet rope from which hung a golden sign.

### *VIP Members Only*

I'd have to figure out a way past that point. A man and a woman in shiny leather bodysuits stood to either side of the hallway entrance. Each sported impressive musculature. The man was a werewolf. He had a distinctive lupine look about him. The woman, though, could have been another type of shifter or another sort of powerful Unusual. I wasn't sure from this vantage point, and I couldn't just stand here and stare at her. It didn't matter who or what she was. She and the male guard were powerful. I wasn't going to force my way past either of them.

Maybe if I'd brought along my sword and didn't have to worry about the rest of the room's denizens, I might have been able to get by. That was nothing more than speculation, though, and pointless. Force wasn't the solution here. Guile was.

I worked my way past the dance floor where scantily clad male and female humans danced for their masters and mistresses standing nearby. The bar was my target. It was the logical place to start in a place like this. Nothing went on in a club without the bartender noticing. I walked up, turned to check that Chip was behind me. I slapped the riding crop against my thigh for good measure to keep up appearances.

He followed the implied instruction and moved a half-step closer.

I decided to tone down the riding crop thing. If I kept this up, I was going to have a bruise on my thigh by the end of the night. Once Chip stood where I wanted him, I nodded approval and turned back to wait for the bartender to make her way down to me. She appeared to be a Naiad, or freshwater nymph. Her kind were classified as lesser Fae, not the high Fae, known by others as elves, like my family. Naiads had powerful magic though, especially around a source of fresh water, like behind a bar with sinks and drink dispensers. She would be formidable if a fight started in this club.

"What can I get you, mistress?" she tossed her long, red hair back over her shoulder and leaned over to set a cardboard coaster down in front of me.

"Give me a good single malt, neat. Oh, and whatever cheap beer in a bottle you have around for my sub."

She looked past me at Chip and chuckled. "Did you raid a college on your way here?"

"He wants to experience the dark side of life." I smirked and shrugged. "Who am I to judge? If he survives the process, he'll have a story to tell for the rest of his puny human life."

The chuckle turned to a laugh. "I haven't seen you here before. Are you just visiting Baltimore?"

"Something like that. I needed a night out and a friend suggested it to me. You wouldn't have seen him recently? He's a Kitsune named Godo."

Her smile disappeared and she stood up straight. "We don't pass along information about our patrons, even to their friends." She popped up air quotes as she said the last word. "I'll be back with your drinks. We don't run tabs. Pay as you go."

She disappeared to make my drink and fetch Chip's beer. I kept a smile on my face, though inside I cursed like a sailor. I'd let her easy demeanor lull me into rushing things and now she wasn't going to give me anything, no matter how long I plied her. There was nothing I could do about it. I'd have to come up with some other way while Chip and I mingled. I waited for my drink and tried to think of other means to get information.

# 13

# Chip

The only thing I was sure of as I followed Rose through the club was someone had to take that damned riding crop away from her. If she snapped that thing down against her leg one more time to get my attention, I was going to yank it out of her hand.

*Easy, Chipster, don't let her get under your skin. You're playing a part here. She's not really ordering you to follow her around like a naughty puppy. It's all an act.*

Of course, that didn't mean she wasn't enjoying herself. I took a deep breath and threaded my way through the crowd around the dance floor to keep up and stay in my proper position just a few steps behind her. To call this place creepy gave a whole new meaning to the word. It was dark and had an undertone that left a palpable aftertaste in the back of my throat. Even the bottled beer, a well-known brand of light ale, had a taint about it.

We reached the far side of the dance floor. Rose stopped at a tall standing table. She set her drink on the two-foot round-top next to the blood red candle in the center. I stopped a few steps away until she snapped that stupid crop down again and beckoned me over with a jerk of her head. I stepped forward, working hard to keep my shoulders hunched over and my head down as I'd been instructed.

Rose leaned close to my ear. "I blew it and went too fast with the bartender. We'll have to figure another way to see if the hunter has been seen here."

"Any ideas beyond just hang out and hope he announces himself?" I couldn't resist the sarcasm. I didn't really have anything to lend to being here. It wasn't like I fit in with this crowd.

"Just keep your eyes open and follow my lead." She waved me back to my previous spot with a flick of her wrist.

I stared past her and met the eyes of a striking African woman with beaded braids hanging down around her face. An ornate necklace hung around her neck. It had colored beads of various sizes and colors. Some appeared to be rough-cut gemstones in addition to the ceramic beads. She looked away from me as quickly as our eyes met, leaving me to look away as well.

My eyes drifted to the right and fell on her companion, a frumpy, middle-aged white male wearing the most ridiculous collection of leather straps. They were arranged in a sort of harness attached like ornate suspenders to an extremely tight pair of black leather short shorts. Something about the man held my attention. He looked vaguely familiar, though I couldn't place where I might know him from. It certainly wasn't in the current outfit, that was for sure.

It hit me like a ton of bricks a few seconds later as my memory connected with the face. If I wasn't mistaken, that was my father's cousin, Gibby, or at least the guy looked just like him. I'd met him several times in my life. The last time was about fifteen years ago at a family reunion held in Elk City. The more I stared at him, the more confident I was that it had to be him. It was weird. He didn't look like he'd aged a day since the last time we'd met.

He raised his eyes from the floor and caught me staring his way. He blinked and his jaw dropped as he recognized me, too. He tapped his female companion on the shoulder and whispered something in her ear. Her head snapped back around to me and then to Rose where we stood opposite them across the crowded dance floor. After studying us for a few seconds, the woman nodded a greeting in my direction and gestured to a dark corner of the club where a collection of booths sat against the wall. One of them was empty.

I called out over the noise of the thumping music. "Rose, I think I know someone here." I moved closer so she could hear me better. "They've seen me, too. Head for those booths in the corner."

"Who?" Rose asked, scanning the crowded room.

"Don't worry about it. They're moving that way to meet us. Go."

She frowned at me but started moving towards the corner anyway.

We reached the empty booth in the corner and there was a brief moment of tension as the two women sized each other up. After a few seconds, Rose said, "You're an Amazon from the Dahomey, aren't you."

"I am," the other woman said. "And you're a Fae warrior. Your aura is very clear."

"Thank you." Rose extended her hand. "Rose Eldersdottir."

"Hangbe." She didn't appear to have a last name.

With the ice broken, Cousin Gibbie reached out and pulled me close in an awkward and slightly sweaty embrace. "Chip, I haven't seen you since you were in high school, I think. It took me a second to realize who you were. You've grown up since then."

Rose blinked in amazement at the two of us. "How do you two know each other?"

Gibbie and I both answered at the same time. "We're related."

Hangbe looked around and said, "Let's get into the booth and sit while we all catch up. It'll draw less attention to us."

I slid in from one side and Gibbie slid in from the other. The two women sat on the outside edges of the booth across from each other.

I got a closer look at Gibbie. He looked exactly the same as I remembered him, right down to his pasty, pale complexion. "You haven't changed a bit in the last fifteen years, Gibbie. How'd you pull that off? You're my father's age, right?"

Rose said, "It's because he's a vampire, Chip. He can't be related to you or your father. He's too old for that." She sniffed the air and cocked her head to one side. "I'd estimate four to five hundred years. You don't quite have the odor of one of the ancients yet."

"It's three hundred and fifty, thank you," Gibbie said. "Give or take a few years. I stopped counting a while ago. And Chip here actually is related to me, distantly at least. I think he's my great, great, great, grand-nephew or something like that."

"Wait," I said. "You're really a vampire? How?" I stared at him, bringing back all the signs from my earlier interactions with him. He'd only ever attended family events at night. He'd blamed it on his day job. He was always cold to the touch and pale as a ghost. Or, it seemed, pale as a vampire.

"I was turned back in the late 1600s in Germany. I managed to keep in touch with some of my family despite my unfortunate circumstances. When my brother emigrated to the new United States a hundred years later, I found a way to follow the family and keep an eye on them. Every second generation, I would turn up in their lives and claim to be a distant Proctor cousin. You're the first to find out the truth about me."

"So, my mom and dad don't know?"

"Nope. I dropped out of contact with them because of the never aging thing. They'd noticed at that last Proctor reunion I attended. But enough about me, what are you doing here and dressed like that? The last I heard about you, you were some big investment guy up in New York."

"That all changed two years ago when Bobby and his wife were killed. I became guardian of their children and discovered the world of the Unusuals." I filled him in about Rose and Lili and how I had been named Guardian to the children. I left out any mention about Sadie's destiny. I wasn't sure I wanted the family vampire to know that much about the kids.

Gibbie eyes welled up when I told him about Bobby and Lili. He grabbed one of the cocktail napkins from the center of the table and dabbed at his eyes until he got control of himself. "I'm sorry to hear about your brother, Chip. I remember him being a good kid."

"He was the best." I left it at that. "So, is this your usual haunt? I'm not judging, just surprised to run into you here."

Gibbie leaned in close, a big grin crossing his face. "No, we're here undercover."

"Gibson!" Hangbe said. "You don't know you can trust them."

"Nonsense, hon, they're family. We Proctors always trust family."

She didn't look convinced, but Gibbie kept going anyway. "Hangbe is with Interpol. We're tracking a shipment of drugged vampire blood that came in from Europe. She thinks someone here is dealing it to local humans. It'll increase their strength and stamina for a brief time, but the drug in it makes the stuff highly addictive."

"Enough about us," Hangbe said. "You never answered Gibson's question about why you two were here. I don't get the sense you're a real couple, so why are you here?"

Rose said, "Since we're laying our cards on the table, maybe you can help us. We're tracking a hunter of some sort. I don't think they're affiliated with one of the clans." She explained about the string of murders Godo had reported and how they might be targeting Sadie now.

Hangbe shook her head. "Why a little girl if all the other victims were women in their 30s? What is it about the little girl that makes her a target?"

"She's special," Rose said. "That's all you need to know. It's our job to protect her and track this person down before they attack again."

"If you've never seen them, how are you going to find them here?" Gibbie asked. "There are a lot of shady characters here."

I said, "I injured them during their last attack. I think they have a serious leg injury. I don't suppose you've seen a man limping around in the club recently while you've been here?"

Gibbie shook his head.

Hangbe did, as well. Then she paused. "Are you sure your hunter is a man?"

"Why?" Rose asked.

"Because there has been an outsider here the last few nights. There's a definite air of the hunt about the way she carries herself. She had a distinct limp tonight when she came in earlier with her rent-a-date."

Rose tensed. "Where is she?" She looked around.

Hangbe nodded in the direction of the VIP rooms down the long hallway. "She hands the guards there a wad of cash every time she comes in and she goes back to one of the rooms at the end of the hallway. When she comes out, she leaves alone. There's never any sign of the human male she entered with."

I looked over at the hallway with the rooms. "You think she kills them and leaves the bodies there to clean up? That's horrible."

Hangbe said, "This establishment skirts the human and Unusual law. It's the reason we're here searching for the drugged blood. I have no doubt they'd dispose of a body for you if you had the money to pay for the service."

"You're a cop," I said. "Why don't you investigate that and arrest her if you suspect that's what she's doing."

"Murder is a local matter. I'm with Interpol and my current investigation could affect many more people than a few male prostitutes."

I didn't like her lackadaisical attitude about the deaths of innocent people down that hallway. If a guy was dying back there, someone should stop it. Of course, whoever that was had to get past the muscle-bound man and woman guarding the entrance.

Rose said, "I respect your priorities. Thank you for the information. It's very helpful. Do you remember if you saw her go back there when she arrived tonight?"

Hangbe nodded. "Just like every other time. The only difference was her limp. She acts like someone with hunter training. I never got close enough to taste her aura, though, so I'm only guessing."

"Come on, Chip." Rose tugged at my arm. "Time to go back and pretend to be into some extra kinky stuff."

"I guess this is goodbye, Gibbie." I slid out when Rose got up. "You should come by and visit us sometime. I'd give you my number but you don't have any place to keep it right now."

Gibbie patted the crisscrossed straps on his chest and laughed. "You're right about that. I will find you. I still have your father's information. I can get yours from him. Good luck on your hunt back there."

"You, too." I turned to Hangbe. "I hope you track this vamp blood down. It sounds like bad stuff."

"Thank you. Be careful with the hunter. She seemed like someone who knows how to defend herself."

Rose said, "I'll take care of her. Chip can watch. She has messed with my family for the last time."

I waved and resumed my subservient role as I followed Rose across the room to the velvet rope sectioning off the hallway from the rest of the room. The hulking man and the muscular woman both moved to block the entrance.

"These are the VIP rooms," the big man said. "They're for members only."

Rose reached down to her knee-high boots. She stopped when both guards stiffened and reached inside their jackets. They were armed.

"Easy, guys. I'm just fetching my cash reserve." She slowly dipped her hand down into the boot and pulled out a folded pile of hundred-dollar bills. "I wonder if I can purchase a one-night membership?"

The woman looked Rose up and down and then glanced at me. "Will you both be leaving together when you're finished, or will he require extra attention?"

"We'll leave together," Rose said. "Though it's nice to know that service is available if I come back. How much?"

"Five hundred. A thousand if you want the extra services."

Rose flipped through five hundred-dollar bills in the stack and passed them to the woman. She slid the remaining money back into her boot.

The man leaned down and unhooked the velvet rope. He stepped back and said, "The last room on the right is available. Enjoy your evening, madame."

Rose snapped her riding crop down against her thigh again and walked up the three stairs into the hallway. I followed behind her. Both guards smirked at me as I passed by. It angered me that they were so callous with people being injured or killed back this hallway, but I kept my eyes on the floor and my feelings under control. It wasn't like I was going to take on those two. I didn't even know what kind of Unusuals they were. They could have abilities that would end a fight with me very quickly.

The snap of the riding crop ahead of me reminded me I'd fallen behind and I picked up my pace to catch up to Rose. It was time to find this hunter once and for all.

# Rose

The Amazon had said the hunter was in one of the rooms at the back of the hallway. I looked back over my shoulder past Chip. The two guards watched us walking to our room. They'd come right away if we didn't go into the correct one. I'd need some time to come up with a glamor spell to conceal the end of the passage from their view before we could start searching for the hunter.

I reached the last room on the right and opened the door. I stepped back in the hallway to make room for Chip to pass by and slapped him on the ass with the riding crop as he went past me for good measure. The woman guard smirked at the gesture. Chip let out a little yelp and jumped into the room to get away from the follow-up swipe. After he went inside, I followed him and closed the door.

"What was that for?" he asked, rubbing his butt.

"I needed to keep up appearances. They were watching us. We have to keep them thinking we're just another pair of deviants playing our little games."

Chip moved to the door and cracked it open to peek outside. He looked down the hallway for a few seconds and closed it again. "They're still looking this way. If they're watching the hallway, how are we supposed to go and find the hunter?"

"I need to work up some magic to mask what we're doing. It'll create an illusion between us and them that appears to be the end of the empty hallway. Then we go out behind it to take out this hunter woman."

"I didn't know you could do that kind of magic," Chip said. "It sounds kind of complicated. You usually get someone else to do the more difficult spells."

"Well, we don't have any of them here with us, so it has to be me. Now be quiet. I need to concentrate." I pushed down my annoyance at him and stood beside the door. After closing my eyes, I drew in my awareness until I focused solely on the pool of mana deep inside. The power necessary to complete this spell was there, but it would come close to depleting my magical energy stores for at least twenty-four hours.

With my mana pool welling up within me, I extended my awareness outward until I could sense the hallway outside. I drew upon my recent memory of the empty hallway as it lay before me while we walked back to our room. With a single word of power, I laid that illusion over the end of the hallway covering up the last two doors on either side.

It had to be perfect and seamless in my mind's eye. Once I released the spell, there would be no way to adjust it. I did my best to align the corners of my image with the actual corners of the hallway. A lone bead of sweat dripped down the side of my face and then my neck. It threatened to distract me from my task, and I snapped my mind back to the spell. I couldn't hold it like this too much longer. My knees had started to tremble just trying to keep me standing upright.

I checked the corners and the image itself one last time and released the spell. My eyes opened and I gasped. The mana energy rushed out of me to fuel the spell's placement. I'd never tried anything this complex before, and the power burned through me as it raced outward. Every nerve in my skin felt as if they had been dipped in acid. I groaned and staggered to the side.

Chip was there in an instant. He caught me in time to steady me on my feet. "Rose, what happened? Are you alright?"

"I am." My voice came out in a croak. I cleared my throat and tried again. "I'm fine. Let me go." I shrugged my shoulders to release his grip on me.

He let go but stayed close. Worry painted his expression.

"I said I'm fine. It was a more powerful spell than I'm used to casting. Give me a second to collect myself." I nodded to the door. "Check the goons at the end of the hallway. See if they noticed anything when the spell dropped into place."

Chip went to the door and opened it just enough to see down the hall. He watched for a few seconds and then closed it. "They're watching the club now, not the hallway. I don't think they noticed."

"Good," I said. I took a deep breath and gathered myself. There was a fight ahead of me and I didn't need to be all wobbly just because I'd depleted my mana. The room had a small bathroom attached to it. I went in and splashed cold water on my face. That seemed to help.

"Rose, if you can't do this, maybe we can come up with another way to get the hunter."

"I can do it." I walked out of the bathroom and reached down and pulled the silver dagger from its concealed sheath inside my right boot. "Open the door. We have to move fast. That spell will only last a few minutes."

Chip pulled the door open. I strode by and walked into the hallway. I checked the guards. It was like looking through a mist, but I could see them standing at the end by the velvet ropes. They were watching the club and not looking this way. So far, so good.

The spell wouldn't cover our voices, so I whispered, "Your cousin's girlfriend said the hunter was down here in one of these last rooms. Check the door next to ours. See if you hear anything before you open it."

Chip went to the door adjacent to ours and pressed his ear to it. He listened for several seconds then reached down and tried the knob. It turned. He opened the door to peer inside.

"Get out, this room is occupied," A male voice said.

"Sorry," Chip replied. "My mistake." He pulled the door closed. "That's not it. There are two guys in there." Whatever he'd seen on the other side of the door, it had caused the blood to drain from his face.

"Are you okay, Chip?"

"Yeah, I just— I'm not sure what I expected, but it wasn't that."

"Take a deep breath. She has to be in one of these two rooms on the other side of the hallway. Get ready. I'll check the next one."

I tried the next to last door on the left side. The room was empty. That left the final door on the left. I listened at the door and heard a loud groan from inside. This one was definitely occupied. I waved Chip over. The only other door nearby was the clearly marked emergency exit door at the very end of the hallway. We'd use that to get away once we'd taken care of the hunter.

I tightened my grip on the dagger in my right hand and tried the knob. It turned. I made the decision to move fast and twisted my wrist while I pushed the door open with my shoulder.

A woman with short-cropped blonde hair knelt half-dressed astride a man tied spread-eagled to the bedframe. A wide bandage wrapped around her upper left thigh. As soon as the door opened, the woman twisted around to see who was there. She held a bloody knife in each hand.

Her eyes met mine and they narrowed to slits. "It's you!"

I didn't know her, but she recognized me. She dove off the bed towards a pile of clothing on a love seat in the corner. I ran to intercept her, leading with my dagger.

"Chip, check the man on the bed." The guy was a bloody mess, and I couldn't tell if he was alive or dead in my quick look that way. I needed to keep my attention on the woman.

I ran at her and lunged with my dagger.

Somehow, she twisted to the side and avoided my blade. Her knife-wielding hand came around and slashed at my extended forearm.

I hissed in pain as the tip of the blade sliced into my wrist. It wasn't deep enough to do too much damage, but it hurt. I managed to keep the grip on my blade despite the pain.

She dodged behind the room's lone wooden chair and leaned back to kick the chair in my direction.

It lifted from the ground and sailed in my direction, causing me to overcompensate as I avoided it. I stumbled to the side.

This wasn't going my way at all. By the time I recovered, she'd made a limping run for the door, dodging past me as I slashed outward with my dagger. For someone with an injury, this woman moved plenty fast.

She burst out into the hallway and turned left to run out the emergency exit. A ringing alarm bell sounded immediately.

"Chip, we've got to go. She's getting away."

"He's bleeding out. I have to stop it."

"It's too late." There was no way anyone cut up like that was going to survive. "Come on, we need to go. The alarm will cancel out my illusion."

Shouts had already started down the hallway's far end where the club was located.

I ran over and tugged Chip's elbow, yanking him off the bed. "Come on. We have to go. NOW!"

We both ran into the hallway. The two bouncers pounded down the carpeted hallway towards us. I pointed at the emergency exit and ran after our elusive hunter. Chip ran along right behind me.

The exit led to a staircase up to the first floor. The stairs opened up into a broad hallway leading to the front of the building. I knew that way was boarded up, so I turned and ran for the back of the house. Down the stairs to the club, the snarls of at least one changed shifter echoed up from below. We needed to get out of here. I gave up on catching the hunter. I didn't think we'd have time to track her down now. We'd have our own trackers to lose.

The hallway led to a broken-down and dusty kitchen at the back of the building. The door into the alley out back was wide open. I ran to the opening and stopped to check and make sure no one waited to ambush us as we rushed through.

Seeing it was safe, I grabbed Chip and pulled him past me to keep him moving. We ran into the alley together and I pointed to the left. "Go, go. We have to get to the car and get out of here. I don't think these people chasing us are going to stop here." I looked back into the house and saw shadowy shapes moving inside coming our way.

When Chip didn't immediately run down the alley, I turned to hurry him along and jerked to a stop right beside him. Someone blocked the way.

"Hello, Rose." The accented voice rolled the R in my name just a little too long. "It has been a while."

I nodded a deferential partial bow in the direction of the vampire lord of Baltimore's Unusuals. He stood at the end of the alley flanked by a pair of his henchmen. One was definitely another vamp. The other was big and muscular, but I couldn't figure out what kind of Unusual creature he was from here.

"Good evening to you, Vincente," I replied. "Let me guess. You don't just tolerate this establishment in your city, you own it, too." The tall vampire had black, slicked back hair and wore a tailored black sport coat and slacks with a black, silk shirt open one button too many.

"If one must keep an eye on certain activities, it often requires hands-on management, don't you think?" Most ancient vampires who'd come to America over the years had lost their old-world accents, but not Vincente. If anything, he'd cultivated his Eastern European accent to be even more pronounced than normal.

"Some things probably shouldn't be allowed to be managed at all in my book." I had run into Vincente before, and he and I had an uneasy truce regarding his baser proclivities. He technically stayed within the expected norms between the Unusual and human communities, but there were many gray areas where he strayed outside the lines I was sure.

A growling huff behind me told me the shifter bouncers from down in the club had come up behind us. I didn't bother to turn around. Vincente was here and he seemed like he wanted something. I was pretty sure he wasn't going to let anything happen to us. The question was, what was it going to cost us?

"I saw you come into the club with your plaything." He indicated Chip standing beside me. "I was almost positive you were there for something other than recreation, but I waited for you to play your hand. Who was it you were after in the VIP rooms?"

"The woman in the last room on the left is a hunter who's attacked my family twice now. That won't stand. You understand that much at least, right, Vincente? Family must be protected."

"But she was a patron in my club and therefore under my protection on neutral ground. If you wanted to attack her, you should have waited until she left."

I shook my head. "I couldn't take that chance. As you can see, she has once again given us the slip. Now she's out there ready to attack us again."

Vincente's eyes grew cold. "That is not my concern. You've presented me with a direct affront to my honor. I care not about this woman you're after. She played by my rules. You are the ones who violated protocol."

I knew I had to play this carefully. I couldn't show weakness, but I couldn't be so bold as to offer insult. With Vincente, it was always how you played the game and not so much what you'd done to piss him off.

"I'm sorry, Vincente. Next time I will be sure of the ownership of an establishment before I attempt to take down a target. Is that a sufficient apology for you, my Lord?"

"Perhaps." Vincente's eyes shifted to Chip. "I sense a hidden, old-world power in this one, but he smells like a human. Tell me your name, human."

"I'm Chip. I guess from the accent out of a bad Dracula movie, you're the head honcho around here."

I froze. Now was not the time for Chip to try out his fast and loose New York style. I studied Vincente to see if I could read his reaction.

The vampire said nothing for a few, long seconds. Then his mouth broke into a broad, toothy grin. "I feel the rising power behind you, but you are an enigma to me, Chip. Luckily, I like puzzles. Perhaps I should take you off Rose's hands for a few days until I figure out the solution to you."

"I'm sorry, my Lord," Chip said. "I have a very special young lady at home who's waiting for me to return tonight. I'll have to come visit you another time. Now, if you don't mind, we'd like to go."

A palpable magical hum filled the air. At first, I didn't know where it came from. Then the hairs on my arm closest to Chip stood on end. What was he doing? It was as if he had poured all his mana into a spell or power of some sort and held it tensed and ready to release at any moment.

Vincente's eyes narrowed and he studied Chip with a dark intensity.

He had to be able to feel the raw power coming from the man standing next to me. After a long staring contest with Chip, he smiled again, this time his lips parted enough to show the long, sharp canines inside.

"I think tonight is not the night for you and me to tangle, Chip. I must determine if it is worth the challenge to my power to find out who you are." He waved a hand and the two thugs standing next to him each stepped back to clear a path for us. "You are free to go, Rose, but you have used up your goodwill with me for the current time. Do not test me again anytime soon. I think it would be best if you stayed out of my city for a while."

"It'll be a shame to miss out on visiting you, Vincente. Until the next time, then. Come along, Chip."

Chip nodded and followed me past the vampire lord and his two underlings. We didn't hurry, keeping our speed at a peaceful evening's stroll pace until we had reached the street out in front of the buildings.

"Rose, could you come over here?"

I glanced at Chip. He wavered and staggered to the left. I stepped over to his side. He leaned on me as I reached out and pulled his arm over my shoulders to help support him. He'd turned paler than I'd ever seen him, and his face had broken out in streams of perspiration.

"What the hell did you do to yourself?" I kept him moving forward. We still had to clear the area before Vincente decided to check up on us.

"I think I held onto my Guardian wall of force power a little too long."

"Whatever it was, it certainly freaked out Vincente. He didn't know what you were doing."

"Just get me back to the car. I think I'm going to pass out."

He was right. I only just got him across the street to the garage and into the passenger seat of the Firebird before he collapsed into unconsciousness. I had too many questions for him, but for now we needed to get out of Baltimore. The questions would wait.

# 15

# Chip

I woke up halfway back to Westminster. Rose drove the Firebird up the ramp onto the highway leading northwest from the city. She'd wrapped a makeshift bandage of gauze around her injured wrist and used both hands to drive as we sped down the road. Clearly, we'd made it free of the vampire and his henchmen.

"I see you're finally awake," Rose said. She looked my way. "How are you feeling?"

I rubbed my hand across my face and through my hair. "How do I look?"

"Like shit. Chip, what you did back there was very dangerous. Vincente is not to be trifled with. He's very old school when it comes to those who cross him."

"At least it worked to get us away." My stomach gurgled and I remembered how much using my mana stores made me hungry. "Any chance we can hit an all-night diner on the way home? I'm starving."

Rose nodded and got off at the next exit. "There's one here in Owings Mills. Let's get some food in you and decide what our next steps are. The hunter has been flushed out of hiding. That can only make her more dangerous."

A few minutes later, Rose pulled the car into a parking spot in front of a shiny and neon-lit diner. She reached back into the rear of the Firebird and pulled out a water bottle and a towel. "Here, use the mirror and clean up your face and hands a little. You've got that man's blood on you. Keep your professor's jacket buttoned, too. That'll hide most of the blood on your shirt."

I flipped down the visor and used the mirror there to wipe at my face with the dampened towel. I had touched my forehead and cheeks with my bloody hands. I managed to get the worst of it wiped away and to clean my hands.

Satisfied, I turned to her. "Here, let me rewrap that and tape it off properly. Where's your first aid kit?"

She pointed at the back seat. I grabbed it and found the adhesive tape and a fresh roll of gauze. I didn't remove the old bandage. That might start it bleeding again. Instead, I wrapped the fresh gauze over it, making it look a lot neater in the process. "There, that'll do better."

"Thank you," she replied. "Let's go and get you some food."

I opened my door and stood up a little too fast from my seat. My vision tunneled into blackness and dizziness hit me for a few seconds. I had to steady myself on the roof of the car.

"Are you all right, Chip? You just got paler, if that is even possible."

"I just need to eat something and maybe get some water in me. That's all. Come on."

I led the way on wobbly legs into the diner. A middle-aged waitress behind the counter gestured to the nearly empty room. "Take a seat wherever you want. I'll be with you in a sec."

Rose led the way to a booth in the corner where she could see both the counter and the entrance. She gestured for me to slide in first. I didn't have the energy to even have a preference for my seat. I slid in and she sat down across from me.

We looked at the multi-page plastic-covered menus. I stopped at the twenty-four-hour breakfast page. That would do for me.

The waitress came over and pulled a pen from her graying hair where it was pulled back into a bun. "What can I get ya?"

Rose spoke up before I did. "Two coffees first of all. And I'll have the chicken and waffles."

The waitress turned to me; her pen poised over the order pad.

"I'll have a ham and cheese three-egg omelet, a short stack of pancakes, and sides of hash browns and bacon."

She smiled. "Hungry tonight, aren't ya, hon?"

"It's been a long evening. Can you bring ice water with the coffee?"

She nodded. "I'll be right back with your drinks. The cook'll have your food ready in a few minutes."

She bustled away and clipped the order slip to an old-school turnstile in the window between the kitchen and the counter area. A man in the back spun it around and grabbed our order to start cooking it.

"Chip, you've never faced a powerful vampire before. You should be more careful with creatures like that."

"I couldn't let him take us, Rose."

Rose frowned. "It was five to two, Chip. As soon as he suspected trouble, he would have sent them after us. We wouldn't have stood a chance. I didn't have my sword and you were defenseless."

"I have more power than you give me credit for. I've been working on refining what I can do. I've learned to shoot an arrow of power with my mind. It's how I wounded the hunter the other day. I could've taken out at least two of his henchmen before he even knew what hit them."

Rose raised one eyebrow in doubt. Maybe I was being overly optimistic, but my bluff had worked. She had to admit that.

"We got away," was all she said. "That is enough for tonight. We've been banned from the city for a while. Vampires like Vincente have long memories. I'll have to come up with a way to earn back our privileges there. But that's something for a later time."

"At least we know what our hunter looks like. That's something."

Rose's puzzled expression didn't make her look convinced. "We still don't know where she's staying or when she'll strike next. I'd have preferred to take her out earlier tonight when we had the chance."

"She was faster than I've ever seen anyone move, except maybe you. Does that make her some sort of Fae or other Unusual?"

"Maybe," Rose said. "There are some human hunter clans that impart increased speed, strength, and stamina on their people. But I didn't see any clan tattoos on her." Rose shook her head. "She was more than I expected when I went into that room. That's on me. I should have been more prepared."

I started to say something but stopped when the waitress returned with our coffee and water. I waited until she dropped off our drinks and went back behind the counter before I continued. "Rose, you can't beat yourself up over this. We know a lot more now than when we went into that club. That's all a big help."

"True. Warren and I have been focusing on finding a man. We'd just assumed it was a male hunter killing all those Fae women across the country. Most killers like that are men."

"What if she's doing this for a specific reason and not just because she likes the kill?" I waited for a second before I continued. "We've assumed she's come to attack us and Sadie, but that doesn't explain all the other deaths. I feel like we're missing something important about her motivations."

"Whatever her reasons," Rose said. "We can't count on her being gimpy anymore. I recognized what she was doing with that man in the room. Blood rites like that are powerful magic that can boost a person's power and enhance natural healing. He was dead so she was close to finishing the ritual. She definitely has enough extra juice to heal up that leg wound once she's alone."

I thought back to the dead man we'd been too late to save. Anger welled up inside. I wanted to stop this woman and deal with her before she had a chance to hurt me or my family. It made me ache deep inside when I thought of using my power to kill her. It took me a few seconds to realize the aching emptiness was my mana well, run dry by my earlier buildup of power.

Rose and I sat in silence and sipped at our coffee. I drank all my water. The waitress came back with a pitcher and refilled my glass three times while we waited for the food. When she finally came out with a tray filled with our orders, I could barely control my hunger.

I grabbed a slice of bacon as soon as she set the small plate down. I savored the salty goodness while I chewed. She set the main oval plate on the table with my omelet, hash browns, and stack of three pancakes.

"Can I get ya anything else?"

"No," Rose said. "This'll be fine."

The waitress shrugged and laid a slip down on the edge of the table. "You pay at the register up front when you're done. If you need anything else, just call me over."

She left as I poured maple syrup all over my pancakes and hash browns. I used my fork to cut through the pancakes and shoved the first bite into my mouth. I kept going until I'd finished half of the food on my plate. It took that long before I began to feel better inside. I knew the food would help refill my mana pool faster. Sleep would help, too, but we had to get home first before I could go to bed.

Rose grinned as she watched me shoveling food into my mouth. "Slow down a little. It'll still be there when you're ready to finish it."

"I don't think I've ever been this hungry before in my life," I said around a mouthful of omelet and pancake.

"Magic takes a lot out of you, especially if you're not used to using it. I should've included some magic exercises in your training routine. That's my fault. I didn't realize you had refined it into some offensive capabilities."

"I sort of learned it by accident when I met Godo for the first time in the back yard." I told her how I'd used my barrier in a concentrated space to throw the Kitsune across the yard. "That's what told me I could shape the force field I create. It took a little practice, but that's how I learned to narrow the field down to a thin arrow of power."

"That's impressive. With a little practice, you might be able to learn to do even more with it. Having more than just a big, invisible wall in your magical toolbox would be useful."

"I'll take you up on those additional exercises for magic when I'm back to myself again," I said. I finished up the last of the pancakes and omelet. My body must have been metabolizing things in overtime, because I still felt a little hungry and wasn't as full as I expected after all the food I ate. The need for sleep called to me the most, though. The kids would be up bright and early in the morning and if we hurried, I might be able to get in three or four hours of sleep before they woke up.

Rose smiled. "You look better than you did when we walked in here. Ready to head home now?"

"Yes." I stood, grabbing the check and walking up to the register to pay the waitress there. I left her a generous tip after she ran my card.

Rose waited at the diner's entrance for me and held the door as I walked outside. There was a definite fall chill in the air, which I appreciated. I liked the changing seasons and this time of year in the fall and spring were my favorites. The cool air had a little of the promise of what was to come, but still carried a bit of the summer's warmth with it.

Rose and I got in the Firebird, and she headed back to the expressway. As she drove, I asked, "What's next with the hunter? Do you have any ideas?"

"I'll get with Warren next. We've seen her so I can give him a description to use around town when looking for her. If we're lucky, someone will remember seeing her and maybe lead us to where she's staying."

"What makes you think she's staying locally?" I asked.

"She's always gotten away from me and disappeared from sight too fast. Warren's been checking the state traffic cameras on the highways out of town. There's no sign she's driving back towards the city. She must be hiding out close to Westminster. The problem is, there are plenty of homes with garages around this area. She could be almost anywhere."

"Hopefully, getting Warren the description will be the ticket to finding her."

"I hope so. I worry she'll try again sooner than later. We might have put enough pressure on her when we located her in the club to force her to do something rash. That's good if we're looking for her. It's not good if we're trying to protect Sadie in the process. I don't suppose you'd consider keeping her out of school until we locate this woman?"

I'd already considered it, so my answer came quickly. "No, Rose. We're not disrupting Sadie's school routine over this unless it's an imminent emergency. I have to be the Guardian here in both senses and it's important for her to have a normal first grader's life right now. It's bad enough she's witnessed several attacks on us at school and at the park. I want her to feel safe. Keeping her locked inside doesn't project our ability to do that very well."

"You're the Guardian," Rose said. Her tone didn't sound conciliatory. She obviously didn't agree with me on this.

I didn't care. This was important to the well-being of the kids.

The remaining fifteen minutes of the ride home passed in silence. Sometimes, that was the best Rose and I could do when it came to disagreeing about how to raise the kids. I knew she didn't like that I was named Guardian. I hope she knew I'd come to appreciate her input, even when I didn't end up taking her advice. I should probably tell her sometime, but I didn't feel like it right now. Right now, my sole focus was to get in my bed and sleep. Ms. McGarry had texted that she'd set up for the night in the guest room. There was no need to wake her up. She'd leave first thing in the morning, and I didn't mind her staying over.

Rose dropped me off in the driveway and left with just a quick wave. I was in bed and sound asleep five minutes later.

# 16

# Rose

I rolled over in my bed the following morning and hissed in pain when I pressed against the cut on my wrist from the hunter woman's blade the night before. It was still wrapped in the bandage Chip had put on it. I suspected it might need a few stitches. I'd see after I got some coffee in me. Maybe my quicker Fae healing would help avoid a trip to the urgent care doctor.

Once the coffee maker was up and running, I searched my nearly empty fridge for something to eat. There wasn't much from which to choose. I pulled out the half gallon of milk and took the lid off to sniff at it. I was surprised to find it hadn't spoiled yet. That settled, I fetched a bowl and a box of crispy rice cereal from on top of the refrigerator.

With a fresh mug of coffee in one hand and a bowl of cereal and milk in the other, I went to my small round table that served as my dining area. The apartment wasn't much, but I didn't need a lot in my life, just a place to sleep and eat the occasional meal. I spent half my time with Chip and the kids when I was in town. That was where I focused my homemaking skills on the rare occasions where they were needed.

I checked the messages on my phone. There was a text first thing this morning from Warren asking about how the night before went. I decided since he was clearly up and interested, I'd give him a call.

After spooning in a big mouthful of cereal, I tapped the name to dial Warren and set it to speaker phone so I could continue eating my breakfast and drinking my morning coffee.

He picked up on the third ring. "I was wondering if I'd hear from you early this morning. How'd it go last night?"

"You want the good news or the bad news?"

"Always hit me with the good news first, Rose, especially in the morning."

"Our hunter is a woman."

His surprise came through in his voice. "Really? I did not see that coming. Did you kill her outright or question her first?"

"That's the bad news. She got away, and I managed to piss off Vincente in the process of chasing after her."

"That's not good. How is Lord Oldy-Moldy doing?"

"He's as big an asshole as ever," I said. "Plus, I now owe him a favor after he let us go last night."

"I'm surprised he didn't make you pay him back somehow on the spot. That sounds more like him."

"Chip showed off a flash of power last night that gave the old vampire pause. It helped us get away clean, but Vincente warned me off going into the city for a while. That means if we need anything there, you're going to have to get it."

Warren chuckled. "Hey, I'm on the clock when I run errands for you and Chip. As long as he doesn't find out I'm working for you, I'll be fine."

"Gee, you're so mercenary all of the sudden," I said.

"Not all of the sudden. You made it clear a long time ago that we were business associates and nothing more. I'm good with that. I could use the cash."

"Good, because you're going to earn it. I want you to spread her description around the Unusual community. Make sure they know she's a hunter who's killed people like us in the past in other parts of the country. She killed a guy at the club last night before we could stop her."

"I hate chasing women. They don't play by a code the way dudes do."

"Careful how you say that, Warren. In case you forgot, I'm a woman, too."

"Yeah," he replied. "But you're just Rose. We've known each other so long now, I know how you tick. That isn't the case when I have to track down some other woman that needs finding."

"Mystery is the spice of life, my friend," I said. I finished the last spoonful of cereal and lifted the bowl to drain the rest of the milk. I'd already finished my coffee, at least the first cup. "Are you up and about already? If you want to come by and pick me up, we can go and talk to Jed Raynor."

"What do you want to see that old Satyr for? The last time we were there, all he did was leer at you and make rude jokes. I thought you were going to lose it and take his head off the whole time."

Warren wasn't wrong about my reaction the last time I'd gone to Jed for help. I shook my head. "He knows more about the underworld around Westminster than anyone else who will talk to us. It has to be him, as much as it turns my stomach to ask him for help."

"I'll be there in ten minutes to pick you up, then. I might stop, though, and pick up some popcorn for the show when you and Jed start sparring again."

"Very funny," I said. "Just come get me. I'll meet you down in the parking lot behind my building."

I grabbed my keys, wallet, and phone and tucked them into my leather jacket's side pockets. I couldn't take my long blade along from the Firebird, but I didn't want to go out unarmed either. I opened a hidden panel in the wall of my bedroom and selected a nine-inch Bowie knife with a silver alloy core beneath tempered steel. The sheath came in a shoulder rig that hung upside down beneath my left arm inside the jacket.

Feeling better whenever I was armed, I left my apartment and went down the hallway to the back stairs that led to the lot behind the building. I didn't have to wait long once I got down there. A plain, gray SUV pulled up and the passenger window went down, revealing Warren inside.

"I'm paying you too much if you just bought this," I said as I climbed in.

"It's a loaner. My truck is in the shop for a warranty repair." He put the car back in gear and glanced my way. "Ready to head to Jed's?"

"If anyone has heard about a new woman hunter in the area, it'll be him." I pointed at the parking lot exit. "He keeps track of all the hot new Unusual women that move into the area. He has a regular group that reports in to him. It's super creepy but no one wants to tell him to stop."

"As long as you're going in with your eyes open, Rose. He's not going to get all leery-eyed staring at me."

I stared at the side of Warren's head as he drove. "I'm a big girl. This is more important than teaching a hundred-year-old Satyr manners."

Warren drove north from town and turned off by the airport into the countryside. Jed lived on a small farm that had a nice vineyard on it. He grew some of the best Syrah grapes in the area. Local wineries competed to buy his harvest each year. The human vineyard owners around couldn't compete with a Satyr when it came to growing the best vintage grapes.

We drove down a long lane lined with rows of well-established vines on either side. The grapes hung heavy on the plants I could see closest to the SUV. It must be close to harvest time. Warren pulled up next to a stone farmhouse and I climbed out. The front screen door opened and out walked Jed. He stood just under five and a half feet tall and had to be the hairiest person I'd ever seen. He rivaled some of the bushiest werewolves I knew. He walked around in his goat legged, horn-headed form most of the time on his farm. He only changed to human form when strangers were around.

He came down the steps and walked a circle around me. "Ring around the Rosie, pocket full of posies, what brings a Fae princess to my homie."

"Really, Jed. Homie's the best you can do? They're going to take away your bacchanalia membership card if you keep dropping rhymes like that."

A booming, hearty laugh burst from the old Satyr. He reached out with a calloused hand and clapped me hard on the back. "That's my girl. You always give as good as you get, Rosie. You've been that way as long as I've known you, which is just about your whole life."

"Some things never change, Jed. I'm actually here because I'm counting on that trait in you, too."

His eyes widened. "Oh-ho, so you came needing a favor from old Jed. Well, far be it for me to turn down a favor for a pretty lady, though you could take off that heavy leather jacket and let me really see how you've filled out over the years." His face turned into the familiar leer I'd come to expect from the old fart.

I bit back an angry retort, kept my jacket in place, and said, "You get plenty of tail, old man. You don't need to be looking at mine."

"True, true, but it never hurts to ask. I never know when the answer will be yes. Now, what is it you need?"

"I'm looking for a new woman to the area. She's from hunter stock, though I think she's clanless at this time. She's got short, blond hair, about my height, and drives a plain black or dark blue sedan. I think she's hiding out somewhere in the area."

"Why would someone like that hide out around here?" He asked. "There's nothing for a hunter to do in this area. None of the Unusuals step out of line and the majority of the humans are none the wiser for it."

"She's wanted in a string of killings from California to here. She's attacked my brother-in-law, niece, and nephew twice now. She needs to be stopped, Jed. That kind of attention can only end up hurting all of us living in the shadows."

He walked past me and stared out over his vineyards for a minute or so. "Hmmm, well, I might know of someone that matches that description. I heard tell of a cute little honey with blond hair that moved into the old Stoneseifer farm. It might be the same girl. I certainly will be sad if you kill her, and you find out you were wrong."

I held up my arm and pulled my jacket sleeve back a little to expose the bandage on my wrist. "I've met her, so I won't accidentally kill the wrong girl. I'll know her when I see her."

"So, you do plan on killing her? You're not going to capture her and hold her for the authorities?"

"She's dangerous, Jed. I'm not taking a chance on her getting away and making another try on my family."

Jed cocked his head to the side, his goat horns poking up from curly gray hair. "Why is she so intent on killing your family, Rosie? I don't know of anything that makes you all more special than any other minor Fae nobles."

Damn, he was too smart for his own good. I had to tread lightly here. I lifted my hands in a shrug. "As far as I can tell, she's targeted Fae nobles randomly all the way across the country. She kills one and moves on. I'll make sure to ask her for you, though, right before I stick my sword through her."

That last bit brought a sinister chuckle from the Satyr. "I don't suppose you'd have Warren here record the fight for me to watch. I love a good cat fight, and who knows, I might get lucky with a random wardrobe malfunction."

"I don't think we'll have time to set up cameras for your viewing pleasure, Jed. You'll just have to settle on your overactive imagination to satisfy your lusts and deviance."

The leering smile never left his face as his eyes tracked down my body. The look sent a shiver down my back and I imagined what it would feel like to sink my Bowie into his neck and press it up into his brain from below.

"Don't bother with me, lass. I'm just saving the image for later."

Ew. I was going to need a shower after my visit to wash off the mere feeling of his eyes on me.

"Come on, Warren. We've got an old farmhouse to check out. Bye, Jed. Stick to growing grapes. It'll get you into less trouble than your other predilections."

"Now where would the fun be in that?"

"The fun would be in still being alive to enjoy it. One of these days you're going to leer at the wrong girl." I climbed into the passenger side of the SUV. Warren was already inside waiting for me. I whispered, "Let's get out of here. He's rubbed me the wrong way one time too many today."

"On it." He started back down the long lane. "I looked up the Stoneseifer property. There are two old farms in that family. Both are currently vacant. Do you have any idea which one she's at?"

"Is one more remote than the other?"

"The one that's closest to here is right up against the edge of a development. Most of that farm was sold to builders a while ago. Just the farmhouse and a few acres remain with the original property."

I thought about it for a second. "What about the other one?"

"That's a few miles farther away but is still in use as farmland from what I can tell from the satellite view on my map app."

I nodded. "That second one, then. She would want to hide out where it's most remote."

Warren nodded and we started on our way to get rid of this hunter once and for all.

# 17

# Chip

I'd barely gotten Sadie off to school on time in the morning. The three and a half hours of sleep I'd gotten after Rose dropped me off was definitely not enough to make up for the exhaustion I felt after expending all that mana the night before. Luckily, Ms. McGarry had breakfast for the kids ready to go before she left. She was a godsend. Whatever Rose's Aunt Allura was paying her, it wasn't enough.

I spent the rest of the day puttering around the house with Addy while occasionally stopping to play with him along the way. We had fallen into a pretty good routine after Sadie left for school. He'd settle in to watch his morning kid shows while I got some much needed housework and chores finished. By the time he was bored with the screen time, I was bored with the housework, too. Then we'd either play inside or out, depending on the weather. Today was a brisk fall day, so we put on our jackets and went out back so I could push him on the swings.

I got more finished after lunch when Addy went down for a nap. I even worked in a quick forty-five-minute nap of my own, though it didn't feel like nearly enough. We both got up when my phone alarm went off telling me it was time to go and meet Sadie at the bus stop.

Addy and I donned our jackets and off we went for a nice walk to the end of the cul-de-sac.

My neighbors, Barbara and Ellie, already stood at the end of the street waiting. Both their younger kids were the same age as Sadie. Barbara had an older child in middle school. I think that one was a girl. Ellie had an older son in fourth grade. A few other parents I knew only on sight had gathered, too, clustered in another small group nearby. I walked over to join Ellie and Barb.

"Hi, Chip," Barb said. She flashed me a warm smile, flirting with me as usual. As the divorced mom in the neighborhood, she'd set her sights on me from the very beginning. She'd maneuvered herself into situations where we'd have to be alone together planning for some community event on more than one occasion.

Ellie took it all in stride and rolled her eyes then flashed me a friendly grin. She had to be the most easy-going person I'd ever met. Nothing seemed to put her off. She was just always friendly. Rose had surmised she was really a secret serial killer, but that was just Rose having an issue with anyone who was happy all the time.

"Hey Barb, Ellie. What's the neighborhood scuttlebutt? Anything juicy going on?"

They both laughed and grinned at each other with a conspiratorial wink. They loved that I wanted to be up on the local gossip with the rest of them. They considered it very unmanly of me.

Ellie said, "I've heard through the grapevine that the PTA president's husband finally left her and the kids for his assistant."

My eyes widened. Patty's husband left her? I knew they were having issues, but she must be devastated. "When did that happen?"

Barbara said, "It's all over the mom circuit, so I'd say within the last few days. You're on the carnival committee, aren't you, Chip?"

"Yeah. Patty and I have been working closely to make some significant improvements over past events."

Barb reached out and hooked her arm in the crook of my elbow. "I hope not too closely. Remember, I have dibs over the other moms when you decide to start dating one of us." She laughed, but her eyes were piercing and reflected the truth behind her feelings about this.

Ellie reached out and tugged at Barb's other arm until she stepped away from me and let go of my arm. "Barb, you know as well as I do that Chip here is spoken for."

"I am?" This was news to me.

Ellie chuckled. "Yes, you are, though you and the woman in question are being super pig-headed about it."

When I returned their humor-filled stares with a blank stare of my own, Barb rolled her eyes. "She's talking about Rose, Chip. The tension between you two sometimes is actually visible. You should both just get it over with."

I shook my head. "No, Rose and I are definitely not a thing."

"Not yet," Ellie added with a knowing expression. "But the way you two already co-parent those two kids of yours, you might as well be married already."

"She's right," Barb said, "as much as I hate to admit it. The two of you would make a cute couple."

"I assure you, even if I were interested, which I'm not, Rose wants nothing to do with me that way."

I started to say more but was saved by the bus pulling up to the intersection. The red-flashing lights came on and the doors swung open. I waited while the kids started unloading. The first graders sat up front and got off first. Sadie was the third kid off the bus, and I walked over with Addy in tow and took her hand.

"Uncle Chip," she said, "I got a gold star sticker today on my spelling test. Mrs. Whitfield said my score was the best in the class!"

I smiled. "That's so awesome, Sadie. We'll have to put your test on the fridge. That's why I bought those new magnets."

"Can we have hot dogs and mac and cheese for dinner tonight to celebrate? Pleeeeease?"

Both Barb and Ellie overheard her and Barb said, "Better get that girl her reward, Chip. A gold star's a big deal in her class."

"I guess we'll have to make a run to the store before dinner, then. I don't have hot dogs or the makings of mac and cheese in the house right now."

Sadie and Addy clapped with joy at the prospect of going to the store.

"Oh, can we help pick out something at the store?" Sadie asked.

"You already picked yours, but Addy can choose something, too." We peeled off from Ellie, Barb, and their kids and walked across the street to our house. I had the keys on me already, so I pointed at the minivan in the driveway. "Load up. Let's get going so we don't have to drive home in rush hour traffic."

The kids piled in and got into their seats. I checked to make sure they were buckled in and ready, then we all headed for the supermarket. One of the biggest surprises of my journey as the kids' Guardian was to find out how much I enjoyed the everyday and mundane things we did together as a family. The grocery store, doing yard work, shopping at the mall, and even just hanging out at the park all held far more joy than I would have expected when viewing parenthood from a distance before I took over with Sadie and Addy.

We parked and got out. I opted to fetch a shopping cart from the collection area in the parking lot. I pointed at the seat. "Ready to hop in, Addy?"

He crossed his little arms. "Too big, Unca Chip."

This had been coming for a while and I smiled. "Okay, but big boys listen and don't run off in the store. If you don't follow the rules, I'll put you in the seat, okay?"

He nodded and reached for my hand. Sadie came over and I let her push the cart, reaching out from time to time to help steer her from hitting one of the parked cars. We got inside and I said, "Now, what were we here to get?" I tapped the side of my head. "Oh, that's right. We're here for a big fish and some fresh Brussels sprouts and asparagus."

"Eww, no, Uncle Chip," Sadie said. "That's all yucky stuff. I want hot dogs and mac and cheese. You promised."

I laughed and reached out to tousle her hair. "I know. I was just kidding. Come on. Let's get everything and get out of here before the big after-work rush."

It took us a little longer than usual with Addy walking instead of riding. We were bound to move at the speed of his little legs. The good news was he liked to run most places, so I was more often telling him to slow down than the other way around.

Twenty minutes later we were ready to get in line to check out. The kids liked to go through the line with the check-out person over the self-service line. They gave out lollypops to little kids who came through.

"Which line should we choose, Sadie?"

"How about the line with the water lady?"

I scanned the people behind the registers, but I didn't see anyone drinking water. "Which one? I don't see anyone drinking water."

"Not drinking water, Uncle Chip. She's from the water. It's funny because she's not happy being so far away from it right now."

I still had no idea what she was talking about but followed her to a line with just one person ahead of us. The young woman behind the register had long brown hair with blue and white tinted highlights dyed into it. That must've been what Sadie meant. Her hair sort of looked like the water when the waves turned foamy.

"Help me put the food on the belt for the nice lady, kids. No, Addy, no candy. You picked cereal as your one thing to get. Help your sister."

He humphed and put the candy back in the rack beside the cart then helped Sadie put things up on the moving belt. The woman ahead of us finished paying and then we were next. I handed the girl my store card to scan. She handed it back to me and noticed Sadie staring at her from in front of the cart.

"What's wrong, sweetie? You look so serious."

"You want to go home." Sadie pointed at the woman. "You should be yourself and go home."

As soon as Sadie said it, a flash of blue light moved from her outstretched hand and touched the store clerk. The instant the light touched her, she changed in front of our eyes. Her face flattened and changed. Gill slits opened in her neck. When she brought her hands up to her changed face, her hands were webbed.

"Oh, my God. What did you just do to me?" The woman started crying.

"Sadie, what did you do?"

"I let her be herself. You're always telling us to be ourselves, right?"

"Change her back." I looked around. Everyone was so busy with their own shopping and checkout that they hadn't noticed the change in the clerk. She'd crouched down to hide behind her checkout counter.

"Why?" Sadie asked.

"Because I said so. Do it, now."

Sadie reached out with her hand and the blue light flashed from her hand once again. The crouching clerk shifted instantly back into her human form. She touched her face and looked at her hands then stood and ran crying out the front door of the store.

I stood staring at her for a few seconds then looked down at Sadie. What had she just done?

"I'm sorry about that, sir." The manager had come over from the customer service desk across the aisle. "I'll finish checking you out. She must have gotten ill suddenly."

"I hope she feels better soon. Don't get her in trouble on our account. It's not her fault."

"Honestly, I hope she comes back. It's hard to find people to work these days." The manager chatted idly about the store while she finished checking us out. She waited while I used my card to pay and then we left the store. Both the kids were silent until we got back to the car.

"I'm sorry, Uncle Chip," Sadie said. "Please, don't be mad at me."

"Sadie, how did you do that back there?" I helped Addy climb into his car seat and buckle in. "I know you can sometimes see what kind of Unusual someone is, but you've never done that before."

Sadie got in her booster seat and buckled up. "I never thought about it before. The water lady just seemed so unhappy standing there and not in water like she wanted. So, I told her to change."

I didn't know how she'd done it, but I knew it was a problem if it became a habit. "You can't do that. Not ever. People don't want to show who they really are all the time. We have to let them hide if they want to. Other normal people might not understand folks who are different from them and be afraid. Do you understand?"

"I guess so." She was quiet for a second while she thought about it. "So, even when someone is unhappy and wants to be their real selves, I shouldn't help them?"

"It's okay to help people, but you should ask them before you do something like that for someone. Most people can change themselves, so if they're hiding, they have a reason."

I waited for her to nod. I smiled and closed the side van door. I got in the driver's seat and stared forward to hide the furrowed brow and frown on my face. If Sadie did this kind of thing in public again, it could go very badly for everyone involved, including us. I needed to try and figure out what this new power of hers was and how we could control it.

Rose might have an idea on where to look for information on this kind of Fae magic. I'd ask her after the kids went down to bed tonight. She'd have an idea of how to proceed with this. She was the Fae expert, after all.

18

## Rose

Warren and I sat in his SUV watching the farmhouse from across the road that ran beside fields filled with soybeans almost ready to harvest. I could sense the near-readiness of the beans in the fields to yield up their harvest. It was part of my Fae connection to nature and one of my more useless skills. If my aunt were here, she would have pointed out how knowing the proper time to harvest crops was one of the reasons early humans consorted with Fae magic. My aunt wasn't here, though, and I didn't care that there was large harvesting combine tractor parked out in the middle of the field.

Beside me, Warren lowered his binoculars. "I still don't see any movement. The sedan in the driveway matches the one you've been looking for, though."

"It has to be her. This place is supposed to be empty. I found the old farmer's obituary online. He died almost six months ago."

"Well, she's laying low if she's home." He raised the binoculars up to stare through them again. "I haven't seen as much as a curtain wave from someone walking by inside."

"It's almost dark. We'll go down the lane with our lights off once the sun's down. That way she won't see us coming." I fidgeted in my seat. I hated these kinds of stake outs. This was what I hired Warren to

122

do. I didn't usually go along. This was a special situation, though, and I wanted to be here in case she started running. She wouldn't get away from me again.

The sun seemed to take forever to dip fully below the southwestern horizon. Once it finally did disappear behind the hills west of the farm, I tapped Warren on the shoulder.

He looked away from the binoculars. "Still no sign anyone is home. There aren't even any lights on."

"Do you think she knows we're coming?"

"Either that or she fell asleep and isn't up and moving yet."

"Let's go and find out. Make sure your headlights are off and head down the lane. Take it slow on the gravel so she doesn't hear us coming."

Warren reached down and pulled a plastic panel off the lower part of the dashboard. He studied a chart inside the panel and then looked down at the opening he'd exposed.

"What are you doing?" I asked.

"I'm disabling the rear brake lights, so they don't light up when we slow down near the house. In my own car, I have them set up on a toggle switch. This is a loaner, so we have to do it the old-fashioned way and pull the actual fuse." He leaned over and glanced back and forth between the chart and the opening. Then he reached inside and pulled out a little plastic tab with two metal prongs. "There, that should do it." He checked by pumping the brakes and checking the rear-view mirror. He nodded and pulled off the shoulder to drive towards the farm's long gravel lane.

We took our time going down the driveway. I watched the house for signs we'd been spotted approaching. There were still no lights on. It puzzled me and made me extra cautious. "Stop here." We were about a hundred feet from the farmhouse's main entrance. "Let's get out and approach on foot. Something doesn't feel right."

Warren turned off the car and we both got out, closing our doors carefully so they didn't slam shut. I hadn't turned around yet when Warren let out a yowl of pain and doubled over out of sight beside the driver's door of the SUV.

I drew my Bowie and ducked down before I worked my way

around in a crouch to the other side. Warren struggled to free his leg from a crossbow bolt pinning his thigh to the metal car door.

A whistling whirring reached my sensitive ears, and I dove to the ground beside the front tire. A pop and loud hiss told me the incoming bolt had struck the tire inches above my head.

I crawled the rest of the way to Warren. He kept grabbing at the shaft sticking out from his upper leg and then cursing and letting go. Wisps of smoke curled up from his palms.

"Silver! The bitch wrapped silver wire around the shaft. I can't pull it out."

I pushed his hands away. "Let me try. We have to move before she zeros in on us again." My hands wrapped around the exposed stub of a feathered shaft. I pulled, trying to go straight out the direction it entered. All I managed was to get Warren to hiss and curse in pain.

"The barbed head is stuck in the door. Hold still, I need to cut the shaft away."

A thudding whump next to my head from the car door told me she'd missed again. I had to get Warren's leg free before she reloaded. I slid my Bowie knife in between his leg and the car door. I pushed down until I met resistance from the wooden shaft of the bolt. Then I sawed back and forth to cut through the thick material.

I counted the seconds, wondering how long it would take her to reload. Cutting through the shaft was taking too long. Then, the knife broke through and Warren fell to the ground. He whimpered and clutched at the injured leg. The silver had to burn like hell. He couldn't regenerate with the shaft in there, but I couldn't pull it free now. We had to get behind some cover.

"Warren, get up." I pulled at his arm, trying to get it up and over my shoulder to lift him. He shifted up onto his uninjured knee and then to one foot. We half ran, half hopped around the back of the SUV until we were on the far side from her line of sight.

I looked off to the right at the house. "Shit, she's not even in there. The shots are coming from the field to the left." I rose up to look through the glass at the dark field full of soybeans. Then it hit me. They weren't ready to harvest yet. But the combine was parked in the middle of them anyway. She'd set it up as a hiding place, a sort of hunting blind in plain sight. "She knew we were coming or saw us casing the place. She's in the combine."

"That's not good," Warren grunted through clenched teeth. "The tire's flat. We're not going anywhere anytime soon."

"I need to get you some medical attention. That wound's not going to heal on its own with all that silver in there. I need to flush her out so we can get out of here and call for help." I looked around for a way I could stay in cover while I circled around to the field. I didn't see anything promising. I was going to be exposed most of the way. Still, there wasn't another option.

"Before you go, pull this thing out of my leg. That'll stop some of the pain at least."

"Oh, yeah, sorry, Warren." I gripped the shaft with one hand and placed my other on the bloody fabric of his jeans next to the wound. "On three. One, Two, THREE!" My shoulder muscles bunched up as I pulled straight back. The shaft slowly slid free.

Warren groaned then let out a sigh of relief when the shaft came out. I held it up to study it. The entire shaft had been wrapped in silver wire. She'd been expecting a shifter which told me she knew who Warren was and what he was doing here.

"Stay here. I'm going to get her or at least make her run again."

He gave me a half smile. "Don't get yourself killed, Rose. I don't want to explain to your aunt how that happened."

"Gee, that's awfully sensitive of you." I moved to the front end of the SUV and judged the distance to the corner of the farmhouse again. It was a long hundred yards and I cursed that I'd stopped us so far away. No help for it now. I took a couple of deep breaths and ran for the stone farmhouse as fast as I could. My legs took long, bounding strides while I bent at the waist to present as small a target as possible.

I made it without drawing any more fire from the crossbow. I crouched down and took a half a minute to catch my breath while I used my enhanced Fae night vision to scan the dark farmyard around me. I kept my back against the stone wall of the house and worked my way down to the far corner closest to the soybean field.

When I got to the end, I took a quick glance around the corner to locate the combine. If she was inside the elevated cab, it was an awkward angle to shoot back this direction at me. I decided to use that to my advantage and cut across the field to come at the large tractor from directly behind. The hunter would have to shoot directly through the glass in the back to get me that way.

Drawing closer with each step, I didn't see any movement inside the cab. That bothered me. Where was she if she wasn't in the big combine? I know the crossbow bolts had been fired from this direction. I reached the back of the combine and moved slowly around to the side, leading with my Bowie in front of me.

The door to the cab was open and swung back all the way to the side. I reached up to grab the bar and pulled myself up to look inside.

It was empty.

I stood there for a second too long. The whizzing bolt came in from behind me in the direction of the farmhouse. It missed my torso by a hand's breadth. It didn't miss my left arm, though. It tore through the meat of my tricep, passing through and ricocheting off the metal housing of the combine engine.

Yelping at the sudden pain, I fell backwards as my arm's muscles reflexively released my grip on the grab bar.

The hard ground knocked the wind from me when I landed. I lay there, knowing the eighteen-inch high soybeans all around me would give me cover for the time being. My right hand came away from my injured left arm. The bloody palm glistened black in the moonlight.

I couldn't stay here all night and there was Warren to worry about. He wouldn't know she was heading back in that direction. The wind whispered in little gusts and the insects of the night buzzed around the field. I couldn't hear anything but that for a few seconds, then I heard the unmistakable sound of a car starting.

With a groan of pain, I rolled over and pushed up on one arm long enough to see the dark sedan race down the driveway. It swerved around the driver's side of the SUV and sped to the end of the lane. It turned onto the main road and drove around a curve out of sight.

She'd escaped me again. It was time for me to reassess who I was dealing with. I'd treated her as a random murderer or serial killer, but she was obviously well trained and prepared for us to come looking for her. She'd been ready to ambush anyone who showed up..

I stood and walked from the field, taking my time so I didn't trip over a random gopher hole or divot in the ground. I didn't need a broken leg at this point to add to the other injuries Warren and I had. By the time I got to Warren, he'd retrieved a first aid kit from somewhere in the SUV and wrapped up his leg. Blood still seeped through the bandage, but it was mostly under control. He helped me wrap my injured arm. I hoped the muscle wasn't seriously injured, but even if it was, I'd been very lucky out there.

I dug in my pocket for my phone. It was harder than it should have been because the phone was in my left front pocket and reaching across my body to get to it was awkward. I wasn't about to ask Warren to get it for me, though, so I twisted and contorted myself until I finally managed to free the device from my pocket.

"Who are you calling?" Warren asked. "Chip?"

"No, we need an ambulance and a tow truck."

"The paramedics are going to ask questions about how we got injured like this, Rose. There'll be no way to hide that we were attacked."

"I know, but we both need more medical care than either of us can provide. There's an Unusual medical crew on duty in the hospital ER most nights. We'll let them deal with it."

He sighed and leaned back against the side of the SUV while I called 9-1-1. As soon as the dispatcher told me the ambulance and paramedics were on the way, I relaxed. My arm hurt like hell. I funneled that pain into my burning desire to track this woman down once and for all. She wouldn't escape me again.

# Chip

My phone chirped as I closed Sadie's door after getting her settled in bed. It had been a long day and I didn't immediately take the time to pull it out to see who sent the message. I still had to clean up the kitchen from dinner and a dozen other things before I could go to bed.

It chirped again and I pulled it out to look on reflex this time. The two texts were from Patty.

*Are you free tonight?*
*To go over the latest Carnival plans, I mean?*

I sighed. After the attack the week before, I hadn't really given the PTA carnival much thought. However, Patty and I hadn't really had a chance to go over my new plans to update the event and we hadn't rescheduled our meeting.

*Sure. Are you bringing Astrid? Sadie is already in bed.*

A few seconds passed by then she replied.

*My mom's here to watch her. I'll be right over.*

I had a moment of panic. The downstairs was a mess. The kids had their toys scattered all over the family room. Some spilled over into the front hallway and the dining room, too. Patty was only a mile away. She could be here in under five minutes. I decided to start by calming myself down and putting on a pot of coffee so I could stay awake to go over the event. Then I started a mad dash to scoop up as many toys as I could carry at a time and toss them in the toy box in the corner.

By the time the doorbell rang, I'd cleaned up the worst of the mess. I dropped the final armload atop the overfilled toy box and walked to the front door to let Patty in. I looked through the window to be sure it was her on the front stoop and then opened the door.

"Patty, it was an unexpected surprise hearing from you this time of night."

She smiled and walked in. "I've been worried about the carnival, and we never did finish our chat about it the other day. I'm sure it won't take long to go over things. Thanks for letting me come over. It's been a long few days and I needed a change of venue."

"Some days are like that," I replied. I led her into the dining room.

She stopped by the dining room table and faced me. "I don't know if you heard or not, but my husband of fourteen years left me earlier this week, Chip. We were high school sweethearts and he decided it was time for him to move on and leave Astrid, Clayton, and me home to deal with it all. So, no, I don't think there are many days like those."

"Patty, I'm sorry. I didn't mean to be coarse in my response. You must be having a rough time." I tried to put on my most caring tone and gave her a gentle smile.

"I'm sure the mom network has been going overtime spreading the word of our particular neighborhood scandal."

"I had heard something, but to be honest, I rarely pay much attention to the gossiping moms." I gestured to a chair beside the one with my laptop at the dining room table. "Sit down. Can I get you some fresh coffee? I just put a pot on when you said you were coming over."

"That would be great. Cream and sugar for me. Thanks."

I went into the kitchen and made two mugs, one for me and one for her. I returned to the dining room and sat hers down in front of her. Then I took a seat and flipped open my laptop. I took a sip of my black coffee and set it down.

"Ew, you drink yours black? How can you stand it like that?"

I laughed. "It's something I learned to like working late nights on mutual fund launches with my team. We always seemed to run out of cream and sugar before the coffee ran out. If I wanted to stay awake, black was often my only option."

"I'd forgotten about your life in New York. It must have been quite a shock adapting to life here in little old Westminster."

"I won't lie. There was an adjustment period. Rose did her best to keep me in line with my responsibilities as a new stay-at-home uncle. It was the kids that pulled me through it, though. They needed me and that became my focus. I've pretty much left that life behind."

"What about the Unusual side of things? I'm sure that must have come as a shock to you, or did your brother clue you in about it when he married Lily?"

"No, that was a shock. The first time I met Sadie's bed troll it nearly gave me a heart attack."

Patty laughed out loud and took a second to compose herself because she kept giggling. "I can just imagine the look on your face. That must've been priceless."

Having her there, I wondered if Patty, a mother to a Fae child, and being Fae herself, might be able to help with what Sadie did in the grocery store the day before. I'd meant to ask Rose, but I hadn't talked with her since it happened.

"Um, Patty, about the Unusual stuff, I did have a question that came up recently. There's still so much I don't know."

She smiled. "I'll be happy to answer it if I can."

I told her the story of Sadie forcing the grocery clerk to shift her form in public and how she could often see through Unusuals' disguises to pass in the human world. Patty's eyebrows shot up as I explained it all.

She waited until I finished and said, "That's a very rare power, Chip. It's a variation of a dispel magic incantation used by the most powerful sorcerers. I've never met anyone who could do it as a basic skill, let alone a child. To be honest, I've only ever read about it in story books. You have to make sure she knows never to do that again. It could cause trouble for her as well as the person she outs."

"I hadn't thought about it harming her. You're right, though. If she walks around exposing Unusuals like that, people will wonder about how she's doing it, too."

Patty nodded. "Did you have The Talk with her about it?"

The way she said it, it seemed like she was referring to something I should understand. "The Talk?"

She rolled her eyes. "What is Rose doing if she hasn't prepared you to have The Talk with the kids? Addy's a little young, but Sadie's old enough, especially with her powers already manifesting in a public way. All Unusuals have to explain to their kids about remaining hidden in the human world. They learn at an early age about the severe consequences of exposing ordinary people to what is all around them. It's a lesson that goes back centuries to days when people like us were hunted down and killed just for trying to live our lives near human settlements."

"Wow, I hadn't thought about all the history. I suppose those crowds with pitchforks and torches in the town square were all based on historical fact. I just never added it all up."

Patty laid a hand on my arm and leaned close. "I'm happy to come and help you talk with her about it. I've already had The Talk with Astrid. There might be questions you won't know the answers to."

I glanced down at her hand, feeling the warmth of it through my sleeve. It felt good to have someone besides Rose to talk with about stuff like this. Rose had a way of turning everything around into a judgement of my parenting abilities.

"I might take you up on that," I smiled and laid my hand atop hers. "Rose is usually the one I turn to for things like this, but she's busy with important things like tracking down that hunter who attacked us."

Patty gave my forearm a gentle squeeze. "Rose is good at certain things, but I'm sure there are gaps in what she can provide for you, and the kids, too, of course."

I nodded and found myself staring into her deep, sapphire blue eyes and I couldn't pull myself away. I didn't want to pull away. She leaned forward and our lips met. The kiss was gentle, warm, and inviting.

A cold chill pressed against my chest, and it took me a second in the midst of the long kiss to realize it was my Guardian charm, the gold shark's tooth my brother had given me. As soon as I focused on it, my draw to Patty melted away. It was like someone dousing me in ice cold water and I shivered a little as I pulled away.

Patty's eyes flashed blue, and they widened in surprise, then welled up with tears. "Oh, my God, Chip, I'm so sorry. I thought you were giving me signals and I just let out my inner charm. I didn't mean to do it."

"Did you just cast a spell of some sort on me?" I scooted my chair back from her.

"It was an accident. I'm a quarter succubus on my mother's side. It's not something I've had to worry about for a long time. My husband was Fae, too, so he was immune. I'm so sorry, Chip. It just released on you before I knew what was happening."

I stood up and ran my hand up through my hair. A succubus fed on sexual energy and there was definitely sexual energy at play here tonight. "I think I've had enough socializing for tonight. Don't get me wrong. I'm interested, but I've only had one encounter with an Unusual in the past and that didn't turn out so well." I didn't need to tell her it was Rose.

Patty wiped at the tears running down her cheeks. She barely held back the sobs just under the surface. I walked with her to the front door and opened it.

She turned on the front stoop. "Chip, I'm so sorry. I never meant to hurt you in any way. You have to know that."

"Let's leave it alone for tonight. I just need a little time to get used to the idea and you're still fresh from your husband leaving. I'll see you at the next PTA meeting if we don't catch up before then. Be safe going home." I closed the door before she turned to leave. I kept feeling drawn back to her deep blue eyes. Even if she was doing it by accident, her mojo was out in force tonight.

I turned and leaned back against the closed door. As soon as she was out of sight, a wave of exhaustion dropped on me like a ton of bricks. If this was what a succubus could do after just a simple kiss, what would her full powers be like if we'd gone further? I stumbled up the stairs and barely made it to my bed. I didn't have the energy to slip off my jeans and sweatshirt. I fell asleep in the position where I landed without even trying to fight it.

# 20

# Rose

Back at my apartment, an itch distracted me from my reading and I, in an absentminded moment, reached to scratch it with my left hand. The pain dragged a tired groan from my throat as the movement pulled on the stitches when I tried to reach out of the sling to scratch my opposite shoulder. The doctor at the ER who'd stitched me up said I'd likely need to get physical therapy for the injured muscle beneath the open wound. He didn't know how fast I healed, so I just smiled and nodded when the nurse went over the instructions for discharge and follow-up.

Healing fast, however, was relative. Warren had a bolt pass all the way through his thigh and he was probably ready to play a vigorous round of basketball this morning. Shifters regenerated, which was a whole different thing from just healing faster than humans. That meant they grew back tissue and bone almost while you watched. As long as he had plenty of protein and calories to eat last night and this morning, he'd wake up pretty much good as new.

My injuries would be mostly healed in about four or five days judging from wounds I'd sustained in the past. Not regeneration, but way faster than a human would experience in the same situation. All of this meant I'd be better soon, but not in time for me to deal with this persistent itch on the back side of my shoulder blade. I got up from my seat on the ratty couch and walked to the doorway into the bedroom. Turning around, I leaned back and rubbed my shoulder against the door frame's wooden moulding. I finally found the edge of one section that had the right amount of angle to dig into my muscular shoulder through my T-shirt and scratch the itch.

I stood there and rubbed back and forth, letting out a satisfied sigh. This felt so good, and the temporary relief took my mind off worrying about the hunter getting away. Again. Dammit, I was better than this. I shouldn't be the one laid up and injured. It should be her. She'd gotten the drop on us, and we'd nearly paid for it with our lives. Warren and I were lucky. That's all it was. She could easily have killed both of us if good fortune hadn't been with us.

My phone buzzed and I walked over to the side table next to the couch. I didn't recognize the number that had sent the text. I opened the screen and my messages to see who it was. My eyes crinkled in delight. It was the bladesmith.

*I have decided to craft a weapon fit for a Guardian in a modern age.*
*Please bring him to my forge at the museum this evening at 8 PM.*

I should probably check to make sure Chip was available, but I didn't want to make the smith grumpy either. I decided to placate the latter. Chip would have to change any plans he had.

*We'll be there ready to assist in any way you need.*

The smith responded with a thumbs up emoji and several sword and dagger emojis. I chuckled to myself. He didn't seem like the type who went in for new tech and communications like that, but then, I didn't know him all that well. For all I knew, he was an avid online gamer with a wicked fast computer rig.

I switched over to phone and called Chip. It rang several times before he picked up. I looked at my watch. It was after the bus picked up Sadie; he should be back home with Addy by now.

"Hey, Rose, what's up?" He said when he finally picked up.

"I just heard from the bladesmith. He wants to see you and I tonight at eight o'clock. Find a way to be there, it's not really negotiable."

"I'll have to try and line up a sitter. That's too late to have the kids out and Sadie will have at least a little schoolwork to do."

"Ms. McGarry is off visiting family in Boston for a few days," I said. "I suppose you could see if one of the local moms would be available to watch them. You'd have to tell the bed trolls to behave and stay hidden."

"I could do that. Bernard and Brunna are sensible enough. They're more afraid of normal people than the other way around."

I smiled. Most trolls got a bad rap in the human telling of fairy tales, but they were really quite docile and liked to keep away from action whenever possible. They could be vicious when cornered or defending their young, but most of the time, they were nice enough. Still, it brought a smile to my face to imagine seeing Barb or Ellie come face to face with either Bernard or Brunna. It would be hilarious.

Chip said, "I'll call around and get someone. Do you want to pick me up?"

I thought about my arm. "Um, it'd be better if you drove."

"Why?" he asked. "What's wrong?"

"We ran into the hunter last night." I filled him in on the previous evening's events. "She got away and I'm out of commission for a few days until this heals up."

"Good God, Rose, you two could have been killed."

"So could you and the kids. We flushed her out of her hiding place. That should have her laying low for a while until she gets her feet back under her. Warren is heading over to the house today to search it for anything she might have left behind when we forced her to abandon her hideout. The important thing is Sadie and Addy are safe."

"Speaking of Sadie, we had something strange happen at the grocery store the other day." He told me about Sadie and the grocery clerk. "I asked Patty about it last night but she didn't know that much, other than to say she thought it was rare magic."

I did a mental double take. "You talked to Patty about Sadie and her magic?"

"I didn't tell her about Sadie's destiny, Rose. I know better than that. I just figured since I hadn't talked to you—"

"You figured you'd try and impress the hot Fae mom you had over for late night coffee?"

"It wasn't like that at all," Chip said.

"Of course it was," I countered. "This is Geoff Federman all over again."

"Who's Geoff Federman?"

"He was a boy I liked in ninth grade. Patty decided she wanted him, too, and promptly used her Fae charms to take him away from me. My powers were slower to manifest than some of the other girls and I was no competition for her."

"Rose, Patty is a grown woman who came over to make sure the upcoming carnival went off without a hitch. That's all."

I could hear the lie in his tone. Something had happened. That didn't matter as much as telling Patty anything about Sadie. "Look, Chip, if Sadie's powers are starting to show this early, that's a sign of her incredible potential and power as she grows up. Most Fae don't start showing their abilities until puberty, or later in some cases. We can't let anything about this slip to anyone else. Do you understand?"

When he didn't answer right away, I said again, "Do you understand, Chip? This is important. If word gets around, some people could start putting things together and come to the right conclusion."

He grumbled something on the phone I couldn't make out. I waited in silence until he finally said, "I'll be more careful. I just figured it was a regular Fae parenting problem. Patty mentioned having The Talk with her. Does that mean anything to you?"

"It does, and I've been teaching Sadie that along with her regular lessons when we're together. I suppose I need to impress upon her the special need to keep hidden for her and Addy."

"What about what Sadie did with the store clerk? Patty said it's a pretty rare power to have. I just thought it was normal Fae kid stuff."

"It's definitely more than that. I'll have to look it up. There's an arcane library hidden in the college library up on the hill."

"If there is, then I can do the research. I'm the one that has to deal with it. You focus on the hunter. I'll let you know what I find. Just tell me how to get into the library and I'll take it from there."

"I'll fill you in tonight when we go to meet the bladesmith. Pick me up at my apartment at seven-thirty."

Chip said, "I'll be there. See you tonight."

He hung up and I set the phone down on the end table a little harder than necessary. I swore a few times for good measure to get the conversation out of my system. Just when I thought Chip had a handle on his Guardian duties, he goes and screws everything up again.

Chip had once again set me on edge. All I could think was what would happen if Patty ever figured out who Sadie really was. Were all of my school nightmares going to come back to life when I was thirty? I wasn't sure I was any better equipped to handle that now than I was then. There was something about Patty that just got to me and kept me from thinking straight.

I decided to put on some reality TV and lose myself in the inane content to get my mind off Chip and the kids. There was nothing I could do with Chip right now.

Around three o'clock there was a knock at my door. I'd dozed while watching TV and it took a second to wake up.

"Who is it?" I called from the couch. I rubbed at my eyes with my free hand.

"Warren."

It was weird for him to show up unannounced like this. I got up and walked to the front door. I opened it and then turned around to go to the kitchen. Warren followed me down the short entry hall and leaned up against the refrigerator. He didn't even have a limp from the injury last night, the bastard.

I started pulling things out to prepare for an early dinner. I needed food to push my healing faster. "What brings you here out of the blue like this? Did you find something at the farmhouse today?"

"I had to come by. You never answered your texts or when I called."

I stopped what I was doing and went into the living room to look around for my phone. I picked it up and activated the screen. I instantly saw a slew of notifications from Warren.

"Sorry. I must have silenced it after I talked to Chip."

He chuckled. "Was it accidentally or on purpose?"

"Probably a little of both." I slid the phone into my pocket and went back to the kitchen. I popped open a container of chicken from the store and dropped two chicken breasts on the sheet pan. I slid it into the oven and closed the door. I set a timer to check them in twenty-five minutes. "Okay, what's so important you had to come all the way over here like this? Did the hunter leave her manifesto behind detailing everything she plans to do?"

"No, in fact, there was hardly anything. But I did find this." He held out a large manilla envelope. "I think she dropped it loading up her car to get away in the dark. I found it laying in the driveway."

I waved and led him over to the small round table and two chairs that served as my dining set. "What's in there?"

"Look and see for yourself." He opened the envelope and dumped out a pile of newspaper clippings and printed news articles covered with small sticky notes.

I used my good hand to start sorting through the pile. They were a collection of articles. Some were about prominent women killed in communities across the country. Others included several earlier articles about each of the women from before. One had been the local beauty queen, and another had an article posted about a girl named prom queen two years in a row when she was in high school. In each instance, the earlier articles had names matching a woman killed in the last year.

"This is her trail of trophies," I said. "Each of these women are the Fae nobles killed by the hunter before she came here."

"Read the sticky notes, Rose. That's the scary part."

I picked up a printed news article from an Oklahoma City news site. The woman had died in a knife attack after attending a local charity gathering. It was chalked up to a random mugging. I leaned in to try and decipher the scrawled note on the colorful paper strip stuck next to the headline.

*Not the Queen Mother*

I looked up in shock. "She's hunting for Sadie. I knew it."

Warren responded with a grim-faced nod. "I looked at all of them. Some of the notes refer back to a longer written note attached to the first killing. It talks about a prophecy that could shift the line of the future Fae queen. There's something about another noble line being selected to conceive the next queen if the first line dies out."

I knew it. "Since Sadie's already born, she's finally tracked her down here to the east coast to try and change history." I couldn't believe all we'd done to keep Sadie's and the family's secret over the years was going to be undone by some distant prophecy from another Fae noble line. "This doesn't change anything. We always figured she was here to come after Sadie. This just confirms it."

"So, what do we do about it?" Warren wasn't the type to sit idly by. He wanted marching orders.

"We need to find this hunter, the sooner the better. It should be easier now that she's flushed out of hiding. Hire extra help and start turning over rocks around town. Someone's got to know something. Start with looking into the reason she chose that particular farmhouse. Maybe there's a connection. The Stoneseifers are an old family in this area. They've been here as long as we have."

"I can do that. This won't be cheap, though, Rose. I'll have to pay extra to pull my usual helpers off their other cases."

"I'll talk to Aunt Allura. She'll come up with what we need. It'll barely put a dent in the family coffers she has hidden on the damned horse farm of hers."

"Good enough." Warren walked to the door and stopped. "You should show all this to Chip. He needs to know what we're facing and what this woman has done to bring her here."

"We've got something important to do tonight. I'll tell him when he picks me up. That reminds me. I need some extra security on the house tonight. Chip's got one of the local moms babysitting while he comes with me. Can you arrange that for me?"

"Sure. I'll take care of it. A few pack mates owe me for some football bets. I'll offer for them to work it off in trade."

"Just make sure they're good enough to do the job."

Warren smiled, showing his teeth. "Always, Rose. I know the stakes. They'll do the job and keep the kids safe."

I nodded and he left, pulling the door shut behind him. I went back to the kitchen table and sifted through the articles and hand-scrawled notes until the timer on the chicken went off. The protein would go a long way to helping my ripped muscle and skin knit back together faster. While that happened, I'd come up with a plan to trap this hunter once and for all.

# 21

# Chip

The doorbell rang and I went over to answer it. As expected, Barb waited on the porch out front. To my surprise, her son, Jonas, stood beside her. She greeted me with a grin and walked in and stopped just inside to stand beside me.

"Jonas, honey, go find Sadie and tell her I have a surprise for her."

He scampered off into the house to find Sadie, leaving me and Barb at the entrance. She leaned against me and pressed her chest against my left arm. I felt the heat rush into my face like it always did when Barb made a pass at me.

I had called Ellie first, but her oldest needed to be picked up at practice and she couldn't come over. That left me few options and Barb was the most convenient despite her penchant for throwing herself at me. I knew the divorced moms in the neighborhood considered me bachelor numero uno. It made the summer block party an interesting gauntlet of promises to come cook for me and the kids and some more overt overtures.

Barb laughed when she caught me blushing. "You're a hoot, Chip. I swear it's so easy to get a rise out of you. Just tell me what the bedtime schedule is, and I'll get the kids squared away. I did tell Jonas he and Sadie could watch that new animated movie with the singing animals. I'll log in on your TV if you don't have it streaming here."

"I'm sure I have it. I'm in deep on all the usual streaming channels." I wasn't worried about Sadie staying up late. It was a weekend night and she and Jonas got along well enough. "Addy will be tired, though, and will need to go to bed soon."

Barb waved off my concern with a hand. "I'll get him to sleep. No problem. I can get the two older kids set up with the movie and then take him up and read him some stories."

I smiled. She knew the routine well enough. Despite her attempts to capture me for herself, she was a good mom to her two kids. Her daughter, Phoebe, was at least twelve and was old enough to be home across the street on her own.

An alarm went off on my watch. I glanced down at the screen. It was the reminder I set to get out the door on time to pick up Rose and get over to the Farm Museum. "I need to get going. There's juice for the kids in the fridge and I just opened the bottle of Pinot Grigio in there if you want a glass for yourself. You're welcome to whatever you can find. I should be back before ten."

"Go and have fun. You rarely get to go out by yourself. You deserve a night out to refresh your Uncle Chip vibes."

I laughed and waved, then headed for the door into the garage. I decided to take my Tesla out. It was rare that I got the chance to drive it. The minivan was better for ferrying the kids and their stuff around town.

The garage door went up and I backed out and headed to pick up Rose. I pulled up in front of her building and pulled out my phone to text her I'd arrived. Before I could hit send, she opened the passenger door and climbed in.

"You're pushing it pretty close, Chip. We don't want to keep the smith waiting."

"We'll get there in plenty of time. It's just on the other side of town." I glanced over at her arm in the sling. "How's that doing? Did you need to see the doctor?"

"Yeah. I went to the ER. The bolt tore the muscle on the back of my arm. I'll be fine by the end of next week, though. Don't worry about me. Now, get going." She waited until I started driving and then said, "We found proof that the hunter is after Sadie."

"So that woman knows who she is?"

"She has to. She had records of all her kills across the country. There was evidence she was looking for the Queen Mother. It was all an attempt to kill the line that would bear the next queen. Now that she's here, she's obviously figured out Sadie is already born. If she can kill Sadie, there's still a chance that crackpot prophecy of hers will come true."

I didn't like the sound of any of this. It wasn't necessarily a surprise, though. The woman had attacked Sadie twice now. "Maybe we should reschedule this and go back home. Barb isn't up to fending off an attack."

"Keep driving. Warren's got some friends watching over the house tonight," Rose said. "This is important, Chip. You've been after me to get you a weapon of your own since we started training together. The bladesmith has made up his mind to do it. That's huge. We can't waste this opportunity."

"If you say so." My mind was on Sadie. I could sense her wherever I was, and she seemed content, even amused based on the emotions I could feel coming from her. The turn into the Farm Museum was up ahead and I figured the sooner we got this over with, the sooner I could be home to watch over my niece.

Rose hopped out as soon as I parked and led the way at a brisk pace. "Come on, Chip, we have to get in before they close the gate for the night." She reached the entrance to the working farm exhibits.

A bored teenager waited there. He held up a hand. "Sorry, ma'am. You'll have to come back another time. We're about to close for the night."

"I had an appointment with the blacksmith. I'm hoping he left a message about it?"

"Oh, you're the ones Mr. Smith said might be by tonight. Yeah, go on in. Do you know the way to his exhibit, or should I take you?"

Rose smiled. "I know the way, thanks." She hustled past the boy, pushing through the turnstile with me right behind her. I gave the kid a half grin and shrugged.

She led me up past the farmhouse and to one of the stone outbuildings behind it. A cheery orange glow came from the open double doors. The ring of a hammer striking metal echoed out into the night.

We entered the smithy and watched as the blacksmith finished up the item he was crafting. It looked like half a black iron hinge. He had the glowing metal on the anvil and used a long metal cone to broaden a hole until it was uniform with the other hole in the long triangular metal door hinge. He doused it in a barrel that hissed and steamed for a few seconds and then pulled it free and set it on a wooden table.

"I'm glad you're on time. We have a lot to do tonight, and I have places to be."

"We respect your time," Rose said. "Thank you for making time to see us."

"Yeah, uh, thank you," I added.

"It's been a while since I crafted a weapon of power. I had to give it due consideration. In the end, I decided based on your status as a Guardian. Such a weapon is a tool of protection and defense. That is something I will complete for you."

I clapped my hands and rubbed them together. "Great, so where do we get started?"

"Take off your jacket and shirt. You can hang them on the back of the chair over there." He gestured to the long wooden table with a single wooden chair in the corner.

The request caught me by surprise, and I looked at Rose, trying to get an explanation from her. She narrowed her eyebrows and nodded at the table across the smithy. I took the hint and followed the instructions. I didn't know the smith well enough to know what it would take to piss him off, but Rose was a different story. It was clear she didn't want me to do anything to upset the process tonight.

I took off my windbreaker and then unbuttoned my shirt. I wasn't self-conscious. I took pride in staying in shape. In fact, I caught Rose stealing a glance in my direction when she thought I wasn't looking. I saw her eyes traveling up from my waist to my shoulders. The grin on my face must have clued her in that I'd seen her looking my way. She flushed and turned her back to me for good measure. It was too late.

I'd already seen her. That alone was worth coming out with her tonight. It was rare to catch her off guard like that.

"Come over here and stand by the forge."

I followed the smith's instructions. The heat coming off the coals raised instant beads of sweat on my chest. At the same time, a cool breeze blew in from outside and sent a chill up my spine.

The smith pointed at my chest. "That is fine work. I can feel the power emanating from it."

I realized he referred to my shark's tooth charm that I'd received when I first became Sadie's Guardian. "Uh, thanks. So, what now? Rose said something about measuring me for my weapon? I assume you need my arm length and stuff like that." I still didn't understand why I had to have my shirt off for this.

The smith grunted something under his breath I couldn't make out.

Rose said, "The measurement is as much a value of your inner strength as it is your outer attributes. Don't worry. It won't hurt. Much."

I turned to look her way. The twinkle of amusement in her eyes almost convinced me she was kidding. Something about the wry twist of her lips told me there might be something else in store for me this evening.

"The weapon chooses you as much as you choose to have it," the smith said. "I cannot make it for you until I see what the Guardian magic requires of me. It is always a challenge dealing with such wild magic. There are many things that might be required of me and you to fashion this weapon."

"Like what?" I asked.

"Let's find out." He reached over to his rack of tools and handed a heavy iron hammer with a short handle to me.

I took it. My arm muscles tensed when he released the weight of it to me. I struggled for a second to hold it at arm's length. I pulled it closer and held it close to my chest. He grabbed a pair of long metal tongs and handed them to me.

The smith pointed at the forge. "I have placed several ingots of precious metals into the coals before you arrived. They are all alloys that might be combined in ways to craft different magical effects. Reach into the coals and draw out the first of them."

My hand's sweat made holding onto the handles of the tongs difficult. I adjusted my grip and reached towards the glimmering heat coming off the banked coals. I couldn't see anything in there, so I just stabbed the end of the flat, paddle nosed tongs into the fire with the ends opened up about an inch.

I met resistance and I squeezed the tongs together around something. I pulled out my prize and held up a glowing ingot of molten metal. What kind of metal it was, I didn't know, but it was going to be part of my weapon.

"Place the ingot on the anvil and start hammering it into shape."

"What shape should I try to make?"

The smith shrugged. "It's not my weapon."

I ignored a short snicker from Rose and laid the ingot on the anvil, holding tight with the tongs. I raised the hammer and started beating at the metal, having absolutely no idea what I was doing. The ingot elongated and formed a narrow, triangular bar.

"Enough," the smith said. He took a second pair of tongs and grabbed the transformed ingot. He held it up to the single overhead incandescent bulb. He stared at the metal and smiled.

I wanted to ask him what he saw, but I didn't think he'd answer me if I did.

He set the gold-colored ingot down on the table in the corner and pointed at the forge. "Again."

Four times total I went through the ritual of grabbing a hunk of molten metal and hammering it into a shape. Each shape was a little different. I wasn't trying to make them match. Instead, I let the hammer and the fall of my arm dictate where the metal was drawn out on the anvil.

"That will do," he said as he took the fourth ingot from the anvil. This one, like the one before it, was a grayish silver in color. The second one had been some copper or bronze alloy based on the dull orange color.

I stared at the four metal shapes I'd created. They didn't look like much of anything. The smith stood by the table staring at them with his hands on his hips.

"What does it mean?"

"I do not know all of it, Guardian. However, the metals are an interesting mix and will be hard to meld into one piece. I will have to think on how this will work. He pointed at the first one. "Gold is a sign of purity and represents clarity of purpose. The second is bronze. That is itself an alloy, a combination of metals. Often that stands for flexibility. The third is titanium and represents a lightness and delicacy in a weapon. The last is platinum and represents strength in a weapon. It is an odd combination, and I will have to let the ingots speak to me as I get started on them."

I set the hammer down on the anvil and laid the tongs on top of it. "So that's it? That wasn't so bad? I knew you were messing with me, Rose."

"There is one more thing," the smith said. He drew a small knife from his belt.

"Hey, wait a minute. What's that for?"

Rose winked at me. "Don't be a big baby, Chip. He just needs a little blood."

"Blood!"

The smith frowned. "I need only a few drops for each ingot. There must be some of your essence infused into the final weapon so it will know who it serves." He held out his free hand. "Give me your hand."

I extended my left hand. He grabbed my wrist in his calloused, iron grip. Before I could object or so much as twitch, he drew the sharp knife across my palm. I hissed at the pain and closed my hand in reflex.

He pulled me by my wrist over to the four shapes on the table. "Squeeze a few drops onto each one. Quickly, while they are still somewhat hot."

I turned my hand so I could hold my closed fist over each piece of metal. I squeezed my fingers against my palm, forcing myself not to wince in the process. A few drops fell from my fist onto the first ingot. I moved on to the next and the next until all four had dark splashes of reddish liquid on them.

The smith handed me a small pile of gauze pads. I opened my

palm and pressed them against the shallow cut there. He then wrapped a roll of white bandage around my hand until it was covered. He tucked the end into the wrappings and nodded. "There. That will hold you until you get home. The bleeding should be stopped by then."

"Thank you. I guess we're finished here, then?"

"You are. I will contact the princess when I have finished the forging. She will assist me with the incantations needed to infuse the Guardian magic into the weapon." He turned away and started gathering the four ingots and placing them into a leather bag with a thong to draw it closed at the top. They clinked together as he let it hang from his hand at his side.

Rose tugged at my arm. It was time to leave. I quickly pulled on my shirt and jacket and followed her out. The museum grounds were deserted. I looked at my watch and my eyebrows raised in surprise. We had been in with the smith almost two hours. I had no idea where the time had gone. It didn't seem that long at all.

"We need to get home. I told Barb I'd be back by now."

Rose said, "You'll be home in fifteen minutes. Just drop me off on the way and go straight there."

My hand ached and I held it up to examine the bandage. "You could have told me what to expect. Why do these things always require my blood?"

"Blood has power and magic all its own. Why do you think vampires seek it out?"

We walked into the parking lot while I pondered all the things blood did in the body. Its importance to life itself must have something to do with its magical properties. I had a little trouble with the steering wheel the first time I grabbed it with my bandaged left hand. I winced a little and switched to my right. Luckily, the power steering made driving one-handed pretty easy. I had Rose home in five minutes, and I pulled into my garage almost exactly at ten.

Barb must've heard me pull into the garage. She opened the door into the kitchen and stared at me until I got out of the car.

"I forgot all about you owning that car until now. You always drive the van."

I laughed. "It's not all that practical as a dad-mobile."

She pointed at my hand. "What happened there?"

"Just a little cut on my hand. It feels better now. I'm sure it'll be all healed up before I know it. Thanks for tonight, Barb."

"Don't worry about it. I'm always happy to help out." She pulled on her coat as we walked into the kitchen. "I'll get on home. See you on Monday at the bus stop."

"Where's Jonas?"

"After the movie my daughter, Phoebe, came over to take him back home. He likes it when his sister reads to him at bedtime, so he was fine with it. I got Sadie settled with no problem." She placed her hand on my bandaged one and gave a gentle squeeze. "If you need help wrapping that up in the morning, call me. I make house calls."

I stammered a mumbled reply and she laughed. She waved and walked out the front door back towards her house across the street. I watched her to make sure she got to her house safe and sound. Then I went upstairs and got ready for bed. The whole process tonight had left me more than a little drained and I wanted to get some sleep to shake off the feeling. I knew I'd feel better in the morning. I lay down in bed wondering what sort of weapons I was getting from the smith. I fell asleep to visions of epic swords and axes from fantasy tales I'd read or seen in movies.

# 22

# Rose

The next two weeks crawled by as an agonizing realization sunk in that we'd lost the hunter's trail. She'd gone to ground, and we had zero leads on where to look for her next. Warren and I had turned over every rock and shaken every tree we could find in the Unusual community to find her. No one knew anything.

Warren had settled in and did the only thing left for him to do. I had more trouble being so complacent, but he was right. We had to wait for her to attack again. That put Sadie and everyone around her in danger. We'd all stepped up our guard over the future Fae queen. I left my apartment this evening on my way to trade off guard duty with Warren. Chip, Sadie, and Addy were over at the school for a last PTA meeting before the big carnival event.

Chip and Patty had been spending more and more time together as the carnival drew closer. Both of them had a vested interest in the event's success. Patty, as PTA president, wanted it as a feather in her cap for when she ran again in the second half of the year. Chip wanted it to succeed because everything he did was successful. His drive to make this year a huge one compared to past events was plain in his singular focus on the carnival and not on the missing hunter.

I pulled into the school lot a little after seven. The sun was just settling down below the horizon. I found a spot open right next to where Warren had parked. He wasn't in his SUV and I looked around to see if he was nearby. I jumped when he tapped on my passenger side window.

"Jeeze, Warren. You gave me a heart attack."

"Sorry. I saw you pull in. I was over in that stand of trees watching the area around the school. It gives a good overwatch position for the lot and the main entrance."

I got out of the car. "See anything?"

"Nope. Just parents and kids going into the school for the meeting. Chip and Patty arrived first. They came together in her SUV."

I bit down a sharp response. It wouldn't do for Warren to know how much this latest development between the two of them annoyed me. He probably already wondered about it, and I wouldn't give him the satisfaction of proving him right.

Warren turned and watched another car arrive. The woman inside parked, got out, and hurried inside.

I said, "Go home and get some rest. I'll take the rest of the night. You can bring me coffee in the morning outside of Chip's place."

He nodded. "I'm beat, I'm not gonna lie. I hope something happens soon. We can't keep this up." He nodded when I didn't respond right away and went to his SUV. The crossbow bolt hole in the driver's door was covered with a square of black duct tape. I'd probably get a bill for that. He got a day rate plus expenses. I guess damage to his vehicle counted as a covered expense.

Warren drove off and I reached into the back of the Firebird and pulled out my sheathed sword. I slid the sheath's clip onto my belt as I walked from the parking lot to the stand of trees Warren had been using. It really was the best place to watch the school. I took a few minutes to set some wards around the trees. A hunter would recognize the value of this position as well. Better to make sure no one snuck up on me while I was on watch.

Once the wards were in place, I found a spot beside a tall oak to sit so I could see the school and the parking lot. I settled down and planned in my mind what I'd do to the hunter when I finally caught up to her. She wouldn't get the better of me again.

Around eight thirty, people started leaving. The meeting must be over. I stood and stretched to work out the kinks from sitting against the tree for so long. I scanned the dark perimeter around the parking lot. An attack could come from anywhere out there and I had to be ready. I alternated between that and checking the front door for Chip and the kids.

It was close to nine when they finally came out. They were the last to leave and the lot only had three cars in it. Patty's SUV sat close to the entrance. My Firebird was parked at the end of the lot closest to me and there was another car over by the school's cafeteria loading dock. I suspected it belonged to the custodian who stood inside the school locking the doors behind Patty, Chip, and the four kids.

My eyes widened when I saw Chip and Patty holding hands. Sadie and Addy didn't seem to care. Neither did Astrid or Clayton. Sadie and Astrid were playing some game with their hands and fingers while they walked along. Both would stop every few seconds and start giggling. I shifted my gaze from them and forced myself to scan the parking lot again. Things still looked clear. I decided to release my wards on the stand of trees and walk down to meet them in the lot. I wanted to scold them about their public display of affection in front of the kids.

Chip saw me coming and wisely let go of Patty's hand. She glanced down when he did and then looked up to see me. A broad grin crossed her face that I wanted to slice off with my sword. I took a deep breath and forced myself to calm my demeanor and voice. I wouldn't give Patty the satisfaction of knowing that her actions were getting to me.

"Hey, Rose," Chip said. "I guess Warren's off for the night?"

"Yeah, he's dragging. I told him I'd cover things until morning." I kept my eyes level, even though Patty reached out and hooked her arm in to hug close to Chip. "How did the meeting go?"

Patty said, "Very well. Chip has things locked down with the carnival ride operator. We're going to have even more than last year. Plus, we'll have more booths and food than before thanks to his hard work wrangling the parents to volunteer."

"Chip is something else when he puts his mind to a project." I swung my eyes back to him. "I just wish he'd focus on his primary responsibilities first. Right, Chip?"

"You've got all that covered, don't you, Rose? I don't think I could do a better job than you do anyway."

"That's not the point, Chip."

Patty held up a hand. "Maybe you two should work this out another time instead of here in a wide-open parking lot."

I stopped and rage filled me as I realized she was right. I'd let my annoyance at the two of them cloud my judgment and I'd let down my guard. I took a deep breath. "I'll follow you back to Chip's house and you can drop him and the kids off there."

I didn't wait for an answer. I walked back to my Firebird and got in to follow them. Once inside, I gripped the steering wheel so hard it hurt my knuckle bones, which blanched white from the blood being forced from them. How dare Patty be right and correct me in front of all of them. That woman had a lot to answer for and now she'd caught me letting my duties slip.

The SUV started and Patty drove out past me to leave the lot. She gave a little wave as she went by. I let out a primal scream. This woman was going to pay for this. There was no way it was going to be high school all over again. I wouldn't allow it.

I'd managed to calm myself down a little by the time they got to Chip's house. They unloaded in the driveway. Patty helped get the kids out while Chip went to the garage door keypad and opened it to go in that way. I pulled up at the curb and got out. I grabbed my sword and walked to the front door instead of going in with the Chip and the kids. I wouldn't give Patty the satisfaction of getting in a last dig at me to end the night.

After unlocking the front door with my key, I went inside and leaned my sword up against the wall by the entrance. I went into the kitchen and met Chip and the kids coming in.

"Hi, Aunt Rose, are you going to help put us to bed tonight?" Sadie asked.

"I am." I put aside my resentment towards Chip and smiled at my niece. She didn't deserve my ire. "Take Addy and go up and brush your teeth. It's late. I'll be right up."

"Yes, Aunt Rose." Sadie took Addy's hand and the two of them skipped into the dining room heading for the stairs.

Chip set his keys and wallet in the bowl by the door to the garage. "Go ahead, Rose. Tell me all the ways I'm screwing things up by having a relationship with Patty. I'll wait for you to get it out of your system."

"I could care less about who you date, Chip. It's the shirking of your duties because of a relationship that concerns me the most. You know the hunter is out there waiting for the perfect opportunity to strike. But you're too wrapped up in your lust for the hot mom of the hour. Patty's only using you to get to me. Once she's done with that, she'll lose interest."

"We're casual, Rose. We've talked about how this will work out. We're going in with our eyes wide open."

I rolled my eyes. "The trail behind her is littered with guys who thought they had their eyes wide open. I don't care about you, Chip. I care about Sadie and Addy and keeping the two of them safe. You can't even see how distracted you are when you're with her."

"I don't need to worry about it, Rose. You're always right there to point out my failings. Who needs a conscience with you around all the time?"

I started to answer but Sadie called down from upstairs. "We're finished. Are you coming, Aunt Rose?"

"I'll be right there." I glared at Chip. "This isn't over."

"Of course it isn't."

With a swallowed groan of frustration, I left Chip in the kitchen and went upstairs to settle the kids in their beds. Both of them were in Sadie's room at the end of the hallway. They each held a book for me to read. Addy's was a picture book. Sadie's was a chapter book. It had been a while since I'd put them to bed, and I figured it would do me good to calm down and wrap up my evening with them.

"So, it's reading time?"

They both nodded.

"You don't think it's too late?"

Both shook their heads.

"Okay, Addy we'll do yours first and then put you down to bed.

Sadie can sit with us and listen while I read it." We all sat on Sadie's bed with me in the middle. Addy's book was about a kid who was afraid of going to the office for a late slip and thought the school secretary might be some sort of monster waiting for him. It was funny and had a cute ending.

When I finished, I took Addy by the hand and walked him into his room. Brunna peeked out from beneath her bed and waved at me. I waved back.

Addy climbed into bed and smiled up at me. "Love you, Aunt Rose."

"I love you, too, Addy. Go to sleep and I'll see you for breakfast tomorrow." I leaned down to give him a kiss on his forehead and then left, pulling the door closed behind me. He didn't make a peep, but he'd always been a good sleeper.

Sadie stood in her doorway holding her book. I smiled and waved her to get back in bed. She climbed in and got half under the covers so she could prop up against the headboard to read. I sat next to her and started reading the chapter marked by a colorful local library bookmark. The story was about a young girl who discovered she was magical and had to learn to control her powers as she discovered the world of magic around her. I found myself drawn into the story as I read. It was a story that could have been about me, or Lili, or especially Sadie.

I read well past the time she fell asleep leaning up against me. I finished the book around midnight and got up. I tucked Sadie in and walked out past Chip's room. He was in bed snoring softly. I must have missed him coming up to go to sleep. I fetched my sword by the door and let myself out to resume my guard duty outside. The night chill further soothed my anger and I let the evening's happenings go to focus on watching the house so everyone inside could sleep in safety. I'd let Chip stumble and fall with this latest romance all on his own. It wouldn't last past the carnival and that was only a few weeks away.

# 23

# Chip

It might have been a normal Saturday morning in our house except that the big day had finally arrived. Carnival Day was finally here. It had been quite an event for the kids to watch from the school's windows on Friday while the carnival operator set up the rides, booths, and food stands in the grassy field beside the building.

I'd opted to pick up Sadie from school last evening so we could see some of their set-up. It was impressive how much they'd accomplished setting up so far having just arrived that morning. The trailers had their big side panels flipped up to expose games and food stands inside. The buzz from the other pickup parents was pretty nice to hear. Everyone was excited and more than a few mentioned to me they were bringing relatives and friends to the event. I knew it was going to be a huge success.

A lot had to get done this morning after I got the kids their breakfast. I had to hit the bakery before heading over to set up. Ms. McGarry was coming over after she prepared Aunt Allura's breakfast to help watch the kids so I could go to the school and oversee the final details. Patty was supposed to meet me there. Her estranged husband had his turn to watch Astrid and Clayton that morning. The Carnival opened at four in the afternoon, and we had a great deal to get set up before then.

Sadie and Addy got to have a treat and sit with their toaster pastries in with the TV to watch their shows. That gave me some time to go over the last few organizational emails before I sent out the reminders to all the carnival volunteers. I also sent another copy of the press release to the local radio station. They were supposed to read it to help support the event. I wouldn't be able to listen and see if they did or not, but it was a nice, free source of publicity to have.

My phone rang and I looked down at it where it lay beside my computer. It was Patty. I picked up. "Hey, I was just finishing up the email to send out to everyone. Is that what you were calling about?"

"No, I really just called to hear your voice. It's nice to know you're on the job, though."

"It's nice to hear your voice, too." I paused then took a leap. "Hey, when all this is over and things settle down, I think we should plan a getaway, just the two of us."

"What did you have in mind?" Her voice dripped with anticipation.

"I thought maybe a weekend trip somewhere warm with white sandy beaches and no kids. What do you think?"

"I think it's a date."

I smiled. "Good, then we'll start planning as soon as the carnival is over."

"I'd like that. Now, about the carnival, I heard back from the car dealership and they're ready to bring over the car for the big raffle this evening at the end of the event. They need to make sure someone is there to take possession when they drop it off. Will you be able to get over there in time to do it? I'm swamped with a million tiny details here at the house."

"Sure, what time were they going to get there?" I asked.

"Between ten and noon," she replied.

"I can do that. I have someone coming to watch the kids around nine. I'll pack up everything I need for the rest of the day so I can stay and work on stuff from there. When do you think you'll be coming over?"

Patty paused for a moment and then said, "Sometime after lunch. I don't have anyone to watch the kids. My ex decided to hang with his secretary instead of me and the kids today."

The anger registered through the phone, and I didn't blame her. The guy was shirking his dad duties big time. Patty deserved better than him in her life.

I said, "Don't worry about it. I've got this. I'll make sure everything is ready to go for the grand opening at four. You can come right before then and help with the kickoff."

"Chip, if you keep pampering me this way, I'm going to have to do something extra special to make it up to you."

"Careful, Patty. I'll hold you to that."

"You can hold me anytime you want, Chip Proctor." A shout from Patty's background distracted her for a second. "Hey, I need to go and deal with the kids. They're bickering more than usual today. They must be feeding on my anxiety."

"Kids are perceptive," I said. "They pick up on more than we give them credit for. Don't worry. I'll take care of it."

Patty disconnected on her end, and I set the phone down. I needed to read through this email one more time before I sent it. I had just finished sending it when the front door opened. I looked up, though I knew who it was. Rose was the only one who let herself in like that. I didn't mind, much. I wanted her to feel like she could come and see the kids anytime she wanted to. Still, with things progressing with Patty the way they were, I might have to come up with something like putting a sock on the doorknob to let her know I was busy.

"Hey, Rose, I forgot you were on guard detail today. For some reason I thought Warren was out there this morning."

"He was," she replied. "A lead came in and I took over so he could follow up on it. He called me a few minutes ago to say he discovered something and he's on his way back to tell me what he found. I figured you'd want to know, too."

"Definitely. I assume it's about our hunter?"

Rose nodded. "At this point I'll take anything that might help us pinpoint her location. We have to assume she's preparing to strike again at any moment."

I didn't disagree with her. Things had cooled off even more since our confrontation about me and Patty earlier last week. With the hunter still out there, we both wanted to keep Sadie as safe as possible. That was why I'd asked Rose to take Sadie and Addy to the Carnival this evening. Rose would come later after the kids had an early dinner. Then they could ride the rides and see all the fun stuff going on. We both agreed Rose was the best option for protection knowing what we did about the hunter.

Addy looked up from the TV and noticed Aunt Rose had arrived. He laughed and ran to her. She picked him up in her arms and turned him upside down the way he liked. He giggled and squealed with delight. Sadie got up, too. She came over and waited until Rose put Addy down to get a hug from her aunt.

"Uncle Chip says you're going to come back later and take us to the carnival."

Rose nodded. "That's the plan. Ms. McGarry is coming by first to watch you, then I'll be back to get you as soon as dinner is finished."

Sadie clapped her hands. "I can't wait. Astrid is going to be there and we're going to ride all the rides like big girls."

"We'll see which rides you can get on when we get there," Rose said. "Some might have requirements that you be this tall to get on." She held out a hand a few inches above Sadie's head.

The little girl frowned. "Oh, I thought I was big enough now."

I jumped in. "You'll be able to ride most of them, Sadie. It might be only one or maybe two rides that you're not big enough for. I'll scout them out when I go over early and let Aunt Rose know."

"Okay," Sadie didn't seem completely convinced my answer was any better. She was a smart little girl. She'd learned some of the nuances of "adult speak" and what maybe really meant.

"Go back with Addy and watch your shows," I said.

"He was watching TV. I was reading my book. I'm almost finished."

I smiled. I loved how much she liked reading. "Then why don't you go and see what happens at the end. Aunt Rose and I are waiting for Mr. Warren to come over and talk with us."

She and Addy returned to the couch in front of the TV and

returned to their shows and book. A tap at the door announced Warren's arrival a minute later. Rose went to answer it and let him in. She brought him over. I nodded at the kitchen so we could have a little privacy from the kids while the werewolf gave his report.

The three of us went in there and Rose asked, "What did you turn up?"

Warren started in right away. "A woman who might have matched the description of the hunter purchased some spell components at an herb shop downtown last night. She came in right before closing with a handwritten list of about a dozen components."

"What kind of components?" Rose asked.

"A strange variety including some that were rare and quite pricey. The woman paid cash and left with everything in a brown paper bag."

"That's it?" Rose crossed her arms. "They didn't follow her? They don't know where she went?"

Warren shook his head. "No. But to be fair, she only partially matched the description. She'd changed her hair color to a dark auburn and wore a lot of dark makeup and foundation. It was only when I made some routine calls this morning that the owner of the shop even thought to mention her to me."

"What did she buy, exactly?" Rose asked.

"I have the list here." Warren held up a paper strip that looked like blank cash register tape with a hand-written list on it. "It's strange. I've never seen this combination of components before. I don't know what it means. Plus, it might not even be our girl."

I thought about the description from the shop keeper and how Warren described her, and something tugged at my memory. I couldn't remember what, but I knew it was her. "It's her. I'm sure. Call it a Guardian thing if you want. This is our lady."

"That still doesn't help us locate her." Rose held out her hand to Warren. "Let me see the list." She took it and studied it for a few seconds. "Some of these rarer components might leave a magical residue when used. I'll call Hitch and we'll see if he can suss out where she's hiding."

"He's still mad at you after the last time you hired him," Warren said. "I don't suppose you've worked that out with him yet."

"No, and I don't have to," Rose snapped. "He wanted a tip, A TIP! He's a two-bit sorcerer, not a high-class waiter. All he did was what I asked him to do."

I remembered that particular incident from the previous year. "Didn't he go temporarily blind after he helped you?"

"Yes, but that was a foreseeable outcome, no pun intended."

"I get that, Rose, but given the fact he literally went blind for a few weeks after he helped you, a tip might have been in order. I always say, pay the help as if you don't want them spitting in your food. You get better service in the long run."

Warren cleared his throat and looked away.

Rose glared at me. "Thank. You. Chip. It's always helpful when you share your rich man wisdom with me."

"Hey, I didn't mean it that way. I just meant…"

"I know what you meant, Chip. We all know you're independently wealthy."

I countered with, "So are you."

"No, Chip, my family has money. When I need it for something important, my aunt sometimes shares it with me. There's a difference. Most of the time, I fend for myself." She asked Warren, "Which shop was it. It's not on the list."

"Molly's Custom Herbal Teas. It's out past the college near the fruit stand."

"Thanks, that'll give Hitch and I a starting point. You stay here and watch the house. I'll be back later to pick up the kids if I don't run into our friend first."

Warren nodded and gave me a half wave then headed for the front door.

"See you, Warren. Thanks for everything as always."

"Anytime."

Rose glared at me until I finally gave in and said, "What?"

"When people like Warren are around, you need to watch what you say, Chip. There's a protocol in the family. We don't question each other in front of…"

"What? The help? You know that sounds a lot like something someone with money would say."

"Just watch it. Someday, they'll be dealing with Sadie, and you need to get in the habit of deference now."

I didn't want a fight with Rose right now in front of the kids so I just nodded to placate her. "Let me know what you find out from Hitch."

"I'll call either way. You need to know what to look for if we fail to find her." She waved to the kids and left via the front door.

I stared at the door after she left, wondering why I let her get under my skin like that. I knew better than to push her buttons, but I felt like she needed a reminder to be nice to people. Her hard edge was going to rub someone the wrong way at some point. I sighed and returned to my laptop and the email on which I had been working. I had to get this sent and a dozen other little details handled before Ms. McGarry got here.

24

## Rose

Finding Hitch proved more difficult than I'd hoped when I left Chip and the kids at home. The low-life sorcerer didn't answer any of my texts or phone calls. That left me with no choice but to hunt him down in his usual haunts around town. It was too early for the bars to open up, so I started with his apartment.

I lucked into a parking spot right out in front of his place on Main Street. He lived in a second-floor apartment there. I went to the door and pressed the buzzer to get into the stairway that led up to the apartments above the shops. I pressed it several times with no answer. Then I got lucky. An older woman came down the stairs and opened the door to leave.

She noticed me standing there and glanced back up to the apartments. "Who are you here to see?"

"Hitch, do you know him?" I reached out to hold the door open for her.

The woman sneered. "Yeah, he's my neighbor. Trust me, you're better off without him. He's a pig and sleeps around."

"I'm not his girlfriend," I replied. "I need his help with a work thing."

"Hitch has a job?"

"He does today if I can locate him. He's not answering his phone."

The woman's face broke into a broad grin. "He doesn't have one right now. Another girl got angry with him and threw his in the toilet. I heard the whole thing yesterday through the paper-thin walls of this dump."

"That explains why he hasn't responded to me. Is he up there?"

"His music's on too loud. That usually means he's home, though sometimes he leaves it on just to annoy me."

"Thanks, I'll go up and knock. He probably can't hear the buzzer."

"Suit yourself." She leaned in close. "But, in my opinion, you can do better, sweetie." She left with a sad shake of her head.

I decided not to argue with her about wanting to date Hitch. It wasn't worth it, and she obviously didn't believe me when I told her the first time. I took the stairs two at a time and turned left at the first landing. I heard the music blaring as soon as I was halfway up the stairs. It left little doubt which apartment was Hitch's.

I banged on the door, rattling the thin wooden panels between me and his apartment. After I used my fist the second time, the door opened a crack and Hitch peeked out around it.

"Oh, it's you." He stepped back and pulled the door open the rest of the way. He wore a stained blue bathrobe hanging open over boxers and a tank top. "Come on in. I'm not expecting any guests, so you'll have to excuse the mess."

The place was a dump. Empty pizza boxes and beer cans littered the floor around a beat-up recliner. A first-person shooter video game was paused on the large flatscreen in front of the recliner. Music blared from a decades-old Bose CD player on the counter in the kitchenette. I walked over and turned off the music so I could hear myself think.

"Hitch, I need you for a job."

He pointed to the video game on the screen. "I'm a little busy. My guild is in a tournament today."

"It's important. I need to find a way to trace some strange spell components back to their owner. I'm hoping you can help me."

"And it can't wait until tomorrow?"

"No, it has to be today. I'm willing to pay extra if you're successful in tracking the person who bought the items on this list." I held up the piece of register tape Warren had given me.

"Double what you paid me the last time and you have a deal."

My jaw dropped. "That's a thousand dollars. I'm only talking about a few hours of work."

"Hey, you need me, not the other way around." He flopped into the recliner and put his gaming headset back on. "I have to get back to this game. Let yourself out and turn the music back on before you go."

He pressed a button on his controller and started into the game again.

I stared at him, visions dancing through my head of me strangling him while he sat in that recliner. After a few seconds of relishing the purple of the strangled face in my mind, I let out an exasperated groan. "Agh, fine, a thousand it is, but you're staying with me for the entire day at that rate."

He glanced at me and then back at his screen. "Say please."

If I could shoot lasers from my eyes, he would have been toast. However, I settled for leveling a steely glare in his direction. "Please, Hitch, come with me and make a thousand dollars for the day."

He paused the game again and set the controller down. "See, that wasn't so hard. Give me five minutes to change."

The one-room apartment didn't leave much room for privacy, and I didn't want to watch him get dressed. "I'll wait downstairs. Hurry up. It's important."

I went downstairs and waited outside leaning up against the side of my car. He took closer to ten minutes to come down and join me. I didn't say anything as I walked around and got in the driver's side.

Hitch climbed in the passenger seat and buckled up. "So, where's this list you want me to track. Most spell components don't leave much of a trace to follow them. You know that, right?"

I handed him the list. "I know, but it's the only lead we've got. This woman is a known killer, and we have to catch her before she kills again."

"I heard through the grapevine you and Warren were looking for someone. I didn't know it was a murder case. Why not let the cops handle it?"

"It's completely supernatural in nature. She's targeting Fae women."

"Oh, that's not good. Okay, let's see what we have here." Hitch used a finger to trace his progress down the list on the paper register tape. His eyebrows rose higher and higher as he neared the bottom. "This is some powerful shit here. They must have cost your killer a ton. I don't even know what this combination of herbs and magic components could be used for."

That didn't make me happy. "I'd hoped you'd be able to help with that part, too. We need to know what she's doing."

"I really don't know," Hitch said. "The good news for you is, two items on this list are powerful enough that I should be able to sniff out the residue in a magical sense and tell you which way she went after she bought them. The witch root in particular should be detectable by someone as sensitive as me."

I couldn't tell if he was being sincere or trying to impress me with his magical abilities. My Fae magic gave me access to spells of warding, defense, and some offensive spells. While powerful, they were limited to where and what they could be used for. I waited for traffic on Main Street to clear and then I pulled out of my spot and started to the herbalist shop where the purchases had been made in the first place.

The lights of several police cars alerted me to a problem when I got close to our destination. There were five marked cars total in the shop's small parking lot when we passed by, all with their lights flashing. I went past the small house that served as the herbal tea shop and pulled into the strip mall a hundred yards farther down the road.

"Wait here, I want to see what's going on. If you want something to do, try working your magic to trace those magical components."

Hitch craned his neck back over his shoulder to try and see what was happening at the tea shop. "I should really come with you and get closer to the initial location of the purchase."

I sighed. "Fine. But keep your mouth shut and let me do all the talking. I should be able to cast a simple charm on one of them to see what's going on. You focus on the tracking part."

We both got out of the Firebird and walked on the shoulder back down the road until we got close to the shop. A county sheriff's deputy saw us coming and walked over to meet us.

"I'm sorry, folks. This is a crime scene. You'll have to go back to your car."

"I was coming here to shop for tea. What happened?" I let a trickle of power infuse my words with a slight charm to loosen his tongue.

The deputy's eyes went into a distant stare for a second and then glazed over. "The woman who owns this shop was discovered by a customer first thing this morning. She'd been shot by a crossbow of all things. It was pretty gruesome. The bolt pinned her to the wall behind the counter and the killer left her hanging there for everyone to see when they walked in."

I'd heard all I needed to hear. The only thing I needed to check on was if Hitch needed more time. Before I released the charm on the deputy, I glanced over at Hitch.

He looked at me for a second then said, "Oh, right, I was supposed to work my mojo."

I rolled my eyes and kept my charm in place for a few more minutes while Hitch closed his eyes and muttered words of power under his breath.

"Hurry up, you moron. I can't hold this spell too much longer. The guy might pee himself or something."

"Almost there. Just have to localize the nexus."

I waited, feeling the strain as the deputy's willpower struggled to regain control. He'd know something strange had happened to him when I let the charm go but would be hard pressed to understand or remember us.

"Okay, I'm good," Hitch said. "We can go."

I released the charm as the warlock said it, watching as the awareness returned to the cop's gaze.

He shook his head to clear his mind and stared at us in confusion. "What are you still doing here? I told you to move on."

"Thank you, deputy. We'll go back to our car like you told us to. Come on, Hitch."

We walked back to the car and got in. I looked over at Hitch. "Which way do we go?"

"No way. She never left the area. Whatever she did with those components, she did it close by. Close enough that she probably spotted Warren when he showed up to get that list. That's why the owner got killed."

"Damn. Can you tell what spell or magic she cast with the components?"

Hitch shook his head. "I need to get closer to where she used them. It feels like it's behind the shop somewhere, but I can't get over there because of all the cops."

"What if I leave you here? I'll give you some cash and you can hang in that cafe right over there. Then you'll be able to see when the police leave."

"I can do that. It could take a while. And I don't have any money."

"I said I'd give you some, that doesn't mean you'll get my credit card to use. It'll be enough to feed you and buy a few cups of coffee. Spend it wisely. Call me when you figure out what the hunter is up to." I dug in my purse and handed him thirty dollars. "That should last you all day if you're here that long. I'll expect to hear from you as soon as you know anything at all."

"But I don't have a phone."

"Damn, that's right. Okay, here's another twenty. Call a cab and come find me. I'll be at East Elementary School at their annual carnival after six. Come find me there when you have something to share."

Hitch nodded, got out of the car, and walked to the cafe. I watched him enter the coffee shop and started up the Firebird. There were a few errands I could run and then I'd have to get over to pick up the kids and take them to the carnival as promised.

# 25

# Chip

The crowds from town had remained steady since the Fall Carnival officially opened at four o'clock. Now that it was after six, more kept arriving as the earlier folks got dinner from the various food booths. There was the usual carnival food, including corn dogs, funnel cakes, pizza, and fries. But the PTA had a booth with fresh pulled pork barbecue and roasted beef brisket. The local creamery had brought their food truck to dispense ice cream treats as well. Overall, things were on track to be the best Carnival event at the school ever. My early count from the ticket booth told me we'd almost double earlier years.

I checked my phone. Rose was supposed to be on the way over with Sadie and Addison soon. Patty's ex had just dropped off their kids and she was taking them around to show them the rides. I knew Sadie wanted to ride everything with Astrid. I'd already bought ride wrist bands for both kids so they could ride as much as they wanted.

There wasn't anything for me, as the committee chair, to do at this point. I'd delegated all the responsibilities to the different booth committees. The only thing I needed to do was to be around in case of any unforeseen problems. My real work would start up when the carnival closed and we had to start counting all the money we brought in. Most of it would be electronic receipts, but enough people still used cash that it would have to be counted and put in a night deposit bag to drop at the bank.

My phone buzzed in my pocket, and I pulled it out. Rose had texted me. She was on the way. I smiled, excited to go around to the rides and attractions with the kids. I'd never appreciated how special it was to experience things for the first time again through their eyes. A momentary twinge of sadness passed over me. I knew how much Bobby and Lili would have enjoyed being here for this, too.

I finished doing a round of all the PTA-run booths to make sure everyone was fine. Then I headed for the parking lot to help Rose unload the kids. I timed it perfectly. The minivan pulled in as I walked out from the ring of rides and booths in the field beside the school. Rose climbed out and I laughed at her expression. It looked like a combination of disgust and boredom.

"I don't know how you drive that thing around all the time when you have a perfectly good sports car in the garage."

I laughed. "It's an acquired taste, I guess. I could loan it to you for a week to see if you get used to it."

"Good gods, no. If I ever get used to driving that thing, kill me. I'll be better off for it."

"I'll make a note of that, though I might need it in writing so I can avoid the murder charge."

This time, Rose laughed. "I'll see if I can round up the Counselor to draw something up for us. Maybe a limited power of attorney for minivan use?"

We both chuckled as the kids climbed out. Both bounced up and down with excitement.

Sadie pointed, "Ooo, a Ferris wheel. Uncle Chip, can I go on it? Pleeeease?"

"That's what we're here for, but we have to split up the time between that and rides Addy can go on, too, okay?"

She deflated but only a little bit. The proximity of the rides, music, and sounds of other kids having a good time overrode her temporary mood shift.

"Hey, Sadie, you're here." Patty walked over with Astrid and Clayton in tow. "Ready to ride all the cool rides?"

"Hi, Miss Patty. Uncle Chip says we have to take turns with rides Addy can get on."

"Why don't we divide and conquer, Chip?" Patty suggested. "I'll take Sadie with me and Astrid, and you and Rose can take Clayton and Addison. You and I can join up later with all the kids and do another circuit before things close for the night. It'll be like we're one big happy family."

I really wanted to hang with Patty, but I promised Addy rides, too, and Rose had other things to tend to. I could see it in her posture. She tensed up as soon as Patty arrived. I'm sure it was because she had to set wards or patrol for the hunter out there somewhere.

"Sure. But Rose has other things planned now that she's dropped off the kids, right, Rose?"

"I do, but I could tag along for a little bit and see the sights."

That surprised me, but I went with it. "Okay, Sadie, you can go with Miss Patty for an hour. Here's your wrist band to ride the rides. Be good and listen to her. Do you understand?"

"Yes, Uncle Chip." She let me wrap the band around her wrist, then spun around and grabbed Astrid's hand. The two of them scampered off with Patty right behind them. Clayton and Addy had crouched down and were making small piles in the gravel at the edge of the parking lot. I took the moment to put on Addy's wristband, too.

Rose turned on me with a scowl on her face. "How are you going to be the Guardian over Sadie if you're traipsing around with Addy and Clayton?"

"I always know where she is and I can tell when she's in danger, remember?" I tapped the side of my head. "Besides, this whole field is barely an acre. I can be anywhere in this carnival inside of a minute."

"Fine, you take the two boys. I'll go and shadow Sadie and your new squeeze."

Rose strode off in a huff, leaving me with Addy and Clayton. I took them by the hand and said, "Let's go, guys. It's boys' night out for the next hour. Let's go and see what kind of trouble we can get you two in."

The two of them squealed and tugged at me as they chugged along as fast as their chubby little legs could carry them. We headed for a ride with little cars that rolled along slowly on an oval track. It was perfect for three and four-year olds. Then I could take a breath and figure out what I'd done this time to piss off Rose.

A half hour later, we'd ridden all the little kiddie rides twice and I was no closer to figuring out Rose's deal. I was about to give up and go find her to work it out, when a voice called out my name from the crowd. I twisted my head around to look behind me and spotted Hitch rumbling up behind me.

"Chip, I'm sure glad I found you. Do you know where Rose is?"

"No, but you can call her. She has her phone with her."

"I don't have a phone right now," Hitch replied. "It's a long story and she has to know what I found."

"Why, what did you find?"

"That hunter you all are looking for, she's here, at the carnival. She has to be."

That got my attention. A shiver passed down my spine and I looked around for the woman we'd seen at the club that night in Baltimore. "Are you sure?"

"It's the only thing that makes sense. She created a doppelgänger potion. That's one of the things she was doing at the tea shop. She can make herself look like anyone, anyone at all."

"Anyone?" I stared around at the hundreds of people around us at the carnival. How could I protect Sadie against all of them?

"One more thing," Hitch said. "Drink this." He handed me a small metal flask from his pocket.

I held up my hand. "No, thanks. I need to keep a clear head."

He pressed the warm flask into my hand. "No, you don't understand. There were other spell component residues at the house. I think she created some sort of temporal control potion. This should counteract at least some of the effects."

"What's a temporal control potion do?"

"Drink it. I don't know how soon she'll use the one she made. It is used to stop or slow time in an area. Depending on her own ability to control magic and the amount of certain components she used, she could affect the area all around the carnival."

I didn't understand but I lifted the flask to my lips and took a sip. My face screwed up involuntarily at the bitter taste.

Hitch raised a finger, pointing it at me in slow motion. His eyes were wide with fear. "Driiiinnnk iiiittt nowwww."

I lifted the flask back to my lips, this time forcing my hand like it was pushing through thick, clear gelatin and not air. I tipped my head back ever so slowly and let the liquid pour into my mouth. Then everything stopped.

# 26

# Rose

I followed Patty and the girls into the carnival, fuming and cursing under my breath as I walked along about ten feet behind them. Apparently, more of my words were intelligible than I thought after I caught a few shocked glares from some of the moms. I toned down the swearing, but it did nothing for my overall mood. Here I was again, playing second fiddle to Patty Peyton when it came to guys. I knew that wasn't completely fair, but I didn't care about fairness in the moment. I didn't have any claim on Chip, but he could have anybody he wanted. Half the single moms in Westminster were after him at any given moment. Why did he have to pick her of all people?

Sadie and Astrid swerved to a giant pirate ship mounted like a pendulum, so it swung back and forth until everyone was nearly upside down. I slowed down and moved so I could see them and the people around them. I didn't see the hunter among the crowd in line for the next turn on the pirate vessel. Patty hustled the two girls into the queue for the next go around. The ship swung back and forth, slowly coming to a stop a few minutes later, and disgorging the previous riders.

The bored carny attendant closed the exit gate and moved over to open the entrance. People surged past him to grab their seats. Sadie and Astrid towed Patty to the last row of seats at the stern of the ship.

The attendant went down the line, locking the padded lap bar in place that snugged down against everyone's thighs while they rode. Then he returned to the control panel.

That was the first of many attractions they rode over the next half hour. We finally ended up by the Ferris wheel. It wasn't large by the gauge of such amusement park rides I'd seen in other places, but it was bigger than anything these kids had seen. Patty looked happy to have a more sedate ride to get on with the rambunctious pair. I took a little devious pleasure in how pale she looked after a ride on the twirling teacups. The kids seemed to love that one, but I saw more than one parent stumble off and barf in the grass behind the ride.

When it came to be their turn, Patty and the two girls took a seat on the Ferris wheel bench and leaned back while the bored, long-haired guy in a baseball cap clipped the safety bar down in front of them. He moved around and turned on the ride until they were at the very top and another open car was available to be filled with the next in line.

Across from the Ferris wheel was a carnival trailer booth. The broad window side panel that closed the opening into the booth had been pulled up and secured above the trailer at an angle with a chain attached to the roof. Inside, behind the counter stood a scruffy woman with frizzy curls of red hair all around her freckled, sunburned face. She ran a game where you could throw darts at balloons on a cork board and have a chance at a prize based on the tag underneath.

Most of the carnies I'd seen that night were pretty active in chatting up people passing by to come play their games. They all had a well-polished routine worked up to entice players to take a chance on the rigged competitions. This one was different, though. She was silent, all but ignoring the throngs of parents and kids passing by her location.

I shook my head. She wasn't going to be in this job that long if she couldn't get people to play her game. Even a lowly carny worker had to meet some kind of quota to keep their minimum-wage jobs. I was sure most of them got a cut from the amount spent in their games and booths. She caught me looking in her direction and sneered at me. She flipped me the bird, then she lifted a reusable plastic water bottle to her lips and drank from it, tipping her head back until it was empty. When she took the bottle away from her lips, green light flashed in her eyes and everything stopped around me.

The silence after hearing the music, beeps, whistles, and loud shouts of laughter from the crowd around me came as a complete shock. Everyone had frozen in place. I tried to twist my head to look around and realized I couldn't. I was frozen, too. The only thing that moved in my field of view was the carny girl in the trailer booth across from me. She bent down and lifted a large crossbow from below the counter.

It was then I realized what was going on. Somehow, she'd acquired the magic to stop time. The horror of it all hit me as I realized my innate Fae magic resistance had warded off some of the magic, but not all of it. I couldn't move, but I was aware of my surroundings. None of the people around me would even know that much. To them no time would have passed when the magic wore off. Even when they discovered their watches and clocks had recorded the missing time, they would brush it off as a strange and totally normal anomaly.

I realized most Unusuals would also be affected by this magic. I could just make out the top of the Ferris wheel out of the corner of my eye. Patty might also be aware of this, partially frozen like me. Maybe she was even more resistant and would be able to react. I tried to see if there was any movement up there, but I couldn't tell from my limited perspective.

Across from me, the carny girl lifted the crossbow to her shoulder and aimed up at the Ferris wheel. I tried to scream, to move, to do anything to stop her, but I was powerless. She sighted down the weapon and squeezed the trigger.

The bolt flew six inches from the crossbow and stopped in midair. Once away from contact with the woman who possessed the magic, the inert bolt got trapped in the spell's effect. When the spell wore off, the bolt would continue to travel at high speed the rest of the way up to the top of the Ferris wheel. There it would strike Sadie and all my hopes and dreams for her would be crushed in one instant.

The carny girl reloaded the crossbow and turned towards me. The sneer returned to her face, and she raised the crossbow to aim it at me. She had to be sure to kill me so I couldn't come after her when time started moving normally again. Maybe she could tell I was aware of her actions even though I was frozen. I didn't know.

The second bolt also froze in midair six inches from the end of the crossbow, aimed directly at my head. I'd never be able to dodge out of the way before it got to me. I was as good as dead if it was on target. I screamed in my mind, trying to force myself to move, not to save myself, but to try and change Sadie's fate, somehow. I couldn't believe this was how it was all going to end.

# Chip

My awareness returned in a blinding flash of pain right behind my eyes. It was like I was hurtling along at a hundred miles an hour and suddenly slammed into a concrete barrier.

"Ow! Shit that hurts. Dammit, Hitch, you didn't tell me this stuff packed that kind of punch."

When he didn't answer even though he stood right next to me, I realized no one else was moving or speaking either. I also didn't hear any of the constant cacophony of the carnival's noises. It was silent, though I could make out distant sounds of traffic from far away.

I looked around trying to understand what was going on and Hitch's words came back to me. The hunter had magic that could stop or slow time. She must have activated it and whatever Hitch had in that flask stopped the effects. That meant the hunter was attacking right now.

Frantic, I looked around in the crowd for Sadie. I could sense her to my right if I concentrated, but the sensation was weak. It wasn't as strong as it should have been if she were this close. I ran in that direction, dodging around the still, frozen carnival goers. I had to get to Sadie and keep her safe.

I ducked under a thrown basketball, frozen in midair next to a game booth, and skidded to a stop. I stood across from the Ferris wheel. My sense of Sadie drew my eyes upward to the top of the ride. She sat at the apex of the wheel between Astrid and Patty. A look of joy filled her face, frozen in time as she sat on the ride she'd wanted to get on most of all.

Motion near the ground caught my eye and I turned to see one of the carnival workers moving in her trailer booth. She wasn't frozen like everyone else. It took a bare second to realize she had lifted a crossbow and leveled it at something to my left. She wasn't aiming at Sadie at all.

I looked to the left and saw Rose standing there, frozen like everyone else. The woman aimed at her and pulled the trigger. The bolt slid from the crossbow and stopped a few inches from the end, frozen in midair but aimed directly at Rose.

"Stop!" I shouted.

The carny worker's head swiveled around, and her gaze leveled on me. She didn't look like the hunter, but I knew it had to be her in her magical disguise. "You! How?"

"I'm the Guardian. I have power all my own. Didn't you know that?" I felt like a little bravado was called for here while I stalled to figure a way to save Rose. I didn't know if she would just cancel the time-stopping spell or if it would expire after a set time had passed.

"You can't save them both, Guardian." She twisted the title with sarcasm as she said it. "When the potion wears off in a minute or so, they'll both be dead."

Both? I didn't understand. I stared at the woman in the booth, looking around her until I saw what she'd done. There was a second crossbow bolt frozen in the air, aimed up at Sadie.

"No! You can't. She's just a little girl."

"Little girl? I don't care about little ones. It's the mother of the queen I have to destroy. I've killed all of the Fae nobles of the right age. These two are the last ones. Once they're gone, the one who will influence the future queen the most will be gone. Then the child will never ascend the throne."

I stared at her, confused at first, then turned to look up at the top of the Ferris wheel, seeing Patty for the first time in a new light. The events of the past weeks, the attacks all took on a new perspective for me. They weren't attacks on Sadie at all. They were attacks on Patty. I had just happened to be there with the kids to stop them from connecting on their actual target.

This woman didn't know which noble family carried the mother of the future Fae queen, so she'd decided to target them all. What a cruel way to see the means to an end. She'd slaughtered all of those other women on the outside chance they might be the right ones.

"What's the mother of the future queen to you?"

"My fallen clan will rise to ascendance, but only if the queen fails to take the throne. My prophecy was clear. If the future queen died, another would rise to take her place. Instead, she must grow up and not be crowned. That meant we had to destroy the one who would place the crown on her head." She pointed at Patty and then Rose. "With these last two Fae noblewomen of that generation, I've achieved my goal at last. Now my family will achieve the greatness they deserve. There's nothing you can do to stop me. Those bolts will fly true and end their lives, sealing the fate of my clan once and for all."

I knew I only had a little time before the time stop spell dissipated. Things would start happening very fast here once the spell ended. When it did, I would be left with a horrible choice. The hunter was partially wrong. I was pretty sure I could use my Guardian barrier to block one of the bolts, but not both. Who did I spare and who did I condemn to die? I couldn't bring myself to face the fact that I would lose either of these dynamic women from my life. Losing Rose wouldn't just hurt me, it would devastate Sadie and Addison at a time when they finally had come to a sort of peace with the loss of their parents.

Losing Patty wasn't any better. It had been a long time since I'd felt this way about someone. My old girlfriend Mia and I had an on again, off again romance that flared up whenever she was in Baltimore on a photo shoot. It never lasted more than a day or two and it had been many months since she'd come down for work. Patty had filled a void in my life I didn't know I had. We had something good going here, even though it was early days after her husband left.

"Time's up, pretty boy. The spell is failing and I'm leaving before anyone knows I was even here. It'll be your word against an empty carnival booth." She sat on the counter with her crossbow in hand and swung her legs around so they hung down in front of the booth's window.

In that instant before time started up again, I saw an opportunity to save both of the primary women in my life and maybe even catch the woman responsible for all those other deaths. I stretched out my right hand, my forefinger pointed at the trailer.

The woman flinched, then laughed when nothing happened. "Failed again, Guardian. Now, you're about to lose everything."

What she didn't see was the arrow of force I'd shot with my targeted power. I saw it in my mind's eye as the power cut through the air, ignoring the time stop spell. The force dart cut through the chain securing the large eight-foot-wide panel tilted up and attached to the trailer's roof. The severed link was clear from my vantage point. She had no idea what I'd done.

The chain hung there, suspended in time for a second longer. Then time started again in a jerk, and everything happened at once.

The big wooden panel swung down as the chain no longer held it up. It swatted the two speeding bolts out of the air as they started toward their targets. Then it finished closing, slamming down on the exposed legs of the woman sitting on the booth's counter. She screamed as the crushing weight broke both her legs.

Rose came to her senses first, blinking as she took in what had just happened. She reacted instantly, as if she'd been watching the whole thing play out. She ran to the booth, pulling at the barrier that pinned the woman in the opening. The whimpering hunter slid out from under the lifted panel, slumping to the ground in a heap. Her snapped legs wouldn't support her at all.

With a balled-up fist, Rose punched at the woman twice until her head lolled to the side and she toppled over to lay on the grass in front of the trailer. Nearby, the Ferris wheel started moving again. Patty and the two girls seem oblivious to the happenings down below, though Patty had a confused expression on her face. Maybe she'd known something was wrong because she glanced at her watch and then at her phone's screen as the wheel carried them around and back up again.

I didn't care. I was just glad they were all safe. Somehow, I'd pulled off a solution to an impossible situation. The relief of it all flooded through me as the adrenaline left me with trembling hands.

Rose came over. "Quick thinking with the trailer panel, Chip. I didn't think you had any other options but to save Sadie and Patty on the Ferris wheel."

I could tell she was fishing to see who I'd have chosen to save if I'd really been forced to pick only one. I wasn't going to give her the satisfaction of getting that answer, especially since I didn't know the choice I'd have made either. I'd been saved by my own cleverness once again.

"I didn't have to make that decision. How did you manage to see when everything was frozen, by the way? Everyone else seemed oblivious to anything wrong."

"My Fae magic resistance left me aware but unable to move."

"Wow, that must have been terrifying."

She winced. "I won't lie. it wasn't pleasant."

People had called the police and a medical team rushed over to help the unconscious hunter. They tended to her wounds as we watched. "What about her? We can't let her wake up and get away."

"She won't. Warren and I uncovered more than enough evidence, especially when combined with what Godo left us before he was killed. We can tie her to a string of murders across the country. She's going to spend the rest of her long life in a series of jails. We won't have to worry about her anymore."

"That's a relief."

We watched as Sadie, Astrid, and Patty finished their ride and were let off the Ferris wheel. Sadie spotted us and ran over, jabbering excitedly about all the rides and how much fun she and Astrid were having.

Patty walked over behind them, still looking a little confused. "Something just happened, didn't it?" She looked over at the people working on the injured carny woman. "Is she okay? I saw that door slam down right onto her legs. It was horrible. I wonder how the panel broke free like that?"

Rose shrugged. "You know all these carnival trailers and rides are one accident away from falling apart. That must have been what happened here." She pointed behind me. "Come on, Chip. I think we need to get the kids home for the night, don't you?"

I remembered Addy and then turned where Rose had pointed. Hitch walked towards us with both boys in tow. They had ice cream cones with drips running down their arms to their elbows.

"What?" the sorcerer said with a big grin. "I had to do something to keep them from freaking out when Chip disappeared from beside them."

"It's all right, Hitch," I said. "They'll be fine. Quick thinking on the ice cream. We'll take it from here."

"I want ice cream, too, Uncle Chip," Sadie said. "It's not fair that Addy had some and I didn't."

"Come with me then and we'll get one while Aunt Rose takes care of some important business here. Coming, Patty?"

Patty took Clayton's free hand. "Yes, Astrid. You can have an ice cream, too. I think we've all earned a little treat tonight."

I was looking forward to putting this chapter of our lives behind us with the hunter finally taken care of. I glanced back at the cluster of police and medical responders. Rose watched us walk away with her hands on her hips. I couldn't help but feel like I'd done something wrong. Then Patty came up beside me and hooked her arm in mine, distracting me from my thoughts of Rose and I put it out of my mind. I was sure it was nothing I couldn't fix later.

# Rose

Warren used his connections with the county Sheriff's office to open an investigation into the mysterious woman injured at the carnival. They found a body matching her description hidden in the woods near the school. That was the real carny girl who'd been replaced by the hunter and her doppelgänger potion. The magic wore off in the hospital and the sheriff units responsible for Unusual criminals took over the case.

Godo's documentation of the crimes across the country turned out to be very helpful for investigators in several states to close some cold cases from the past year. I had an itch to sneak into the hospital and finish her off once and for all. If she somehow got off, she'd be back out on the street and start her murderous rampage all over again. I had to trust it was good enough that she'd pay the price in the courts for her crimes, starting here in Maryland for the murder of the carnival worker. If she got off here for some reason, she'd be extradited to other states for her crimes there. This woman wasn't seeing daylight any time soon.

On the way to Chip's for my errand, I stopped by Hitch's place. He still didn't have a phone, so I needed to see him in person to settle up for all his help. I figured he was waiting for me to pay him before he purchased a new one. He met me at the door to his apartment, once again standing there in his boxers, stained white tank top, and the shabby open bath robe.

"Rose, I hope you came with the money you owe me. My landlord is getting testy with my excuses."

"I have it all here as we agreed to." I handed him an envelope full of cash. "Don't spend it all in one place. I added a little extra since you went above and beyond on this one."

That surprised him. "Really, Rose? I don't think I've ever seen gratitude from you before. It's a new look on you."

"Don't get used to it," I said. "This is just because you had the presence of mind to give Chip the counter-spell in that flask. He told me all about it. It was the right thing to do."

"I'm glad it worked. I wasn't sure when I concocted the mixture. It was maybe a fifty-fifty chance at best."

I didn't like those odds, but I wasn't going to quibble with him. "Even so, there's your money. I'm glad it worked out, too. I'll be in touch if I need anything else."

Hitch started to close his door then said, "What's the deal with Chip, Rose? He's more than just a human with some extra powers. There's something else going on here with him and the kids, isn't there?"

I stopped at the top of the stairs and met Hitch's eyes. I let the power flash behind my emerald green irises. "Drop it, Hitch. Don't ever ask me or anyone else that question again. Do you understand?"

"Uh, yeah, sure, Rose. But you know I can be trusted, right?"

"I just asked you something. Do you understand?"

Hitch held up his hand, palm out. "Never mind. Rose. I don't want to know."

I nodded. "Good answer." I waited until he closed the door before I continued down the stairs. I hoped he didn't start asking awkward questions around town about Chip and magic. I didn't want to have to do anything to Hitch to keep him quiet. I'd have to be more careful when involving him in things down the road.

I got back in the Firebird and drove outside of town to the development where Chip and the kids lived. I turned into the cul-de-sac and stopped for a second on the curb out front. Patty's SUV was parked next to the minivan in the driveway. I really didn't want to deal with the two of them together like this. They both acted like it was all fine, but that was because I didn't let Chip see what him being with Patty meant to me. Of all the women he could be with, why did it have to be her?

The front door opened, and Sadie walked out. She must have seen me out the front window. "Come on in, Aunt Rose," she called. "Everyone is here."

I waved back at her and sighed. Time to put on my happy face. I committed to taking it out on Chip in our next session in the dojo. For now, though, I had to stay since Sadie had seen me. I had brought a gift for him, and I needed to pass it along. The bladesmith had contacted me that morning. The weapon was done, and I had picked it up.

The package wrapped in brown paper and twine stood up behind my seat. I put the car in park and got out, retrieved the package and tucked it under my arm.

Sadie clapped her hands when she saw me carrying something. "Is that for me?"

"No," I said. I walked up to the front door. "It's for your uncle."

"Uncle Chip! Aunt Rose is here, she has a present for you."

I steeled myself to face Chip and Patty together and walked inside. It was time to get used to the new normal. Hopefully, it was just a passing phase. We had a lot of years together to raise this little girl to be the queen she was destined to be.

Read the exclusive story **_Guardian's Test_** when Rose first tests Chip to become Sadie's Guardian, and join Jamie Davis' email newsletter.

Get the next book, _Field Trip Fae,_
_book 3 in Uncle Chip Saves the Fae_

# Also by Jamie Davis

**Get a free book and updates for new books.**

**visit JamieDavisBooks.com/send-free-book/**

## Extreme Medical Services Series

(A 9-book Urban Fantasy series starting with)

Book 1 - Extreme Medical Services

—

## Eldara Sister Series

*The Nightingale's Angel*

*Blue and Gray Angel*

—

## Uncle Chip Saves the Fae Series

(An Urban Fantasy Romp Set it the Extreme Medical Universe)

*Book 1 - Unlikely Guardian*

—

## Lone Wolf Squadron Series

(a 9-book Space Western series starting with)

*Marshal the Stars*

—

## The Huntress Clan Saga

(A 6-book Urban Fantasy series starting with)

*Huntress Initiate*

—

## The Broken Throne Series

(A 5-Book Dystopian Urban Fantasy

starting with)

## Help the Author

**I Need Your Help ...**

Without reviews indie books like this one are almost impossible to market.

Leaving a review will only take a minute — it doesn't have to be long or involved, just a sentence or two that tells people what you liked about the book, to help other readers know why they might like it, too. It also helps me write more of what you love.

**The truth is, VERY few readers leave reviews. Please help me out by being the exception.**

Thank you in advance!

Jamie Davis

# About the Author

Jamie Davis, RN, NRP, B.A., A.S., is a nationally recognized medical educator who began educating new emergency responders as a training officer for his local EMS program. As a media producer, he has been recognized for the MedicCast Podcast (MedicCast.com/blog), a weekly program for emergency medical providers like EMTs and paramedics, and the Nursing Show, a similar program for nurses and nursing students. His programs and resources have been downloaded over 6 million times by listeners and viewers.

Jamie lives and writes at his home in Maryland. He lives in the woods with his wife, three children, and a dog.

*Follow Jamie Online*
www.jamiedavisbooks.com